*This is Caryl Chessman's fourth
book, his only work of fiction. We
print it just as we received it from
San Quentin. In it, the author of
Cell 2455 Death Row creates a
character who has reason to hate
the world, and who spends his
brief adult life courting death . . .*

The Kid Was A Killer

Caryl Chessman

WILDSIDE PRESS

For
FUZZY
who, in another day, knew
another kid, who loved him,
and tried to make him whole.

Introduction

by

H. Peter Laqueur, M.D.

> (Dr. Laqueur is a member of the Psychiatric
> Staff of Mt. Sinai Hospital in New York City,
> and a specialist in insulin treatment for schizo-
> phrenics at Creedmoor State Hospital in Queens
> County, New York.)

Death is one of the fundamental phenomena of the universe.
It comes to all creatures at the point where the external
environmental forces exceed the powers of adaptation and
adjustment built into the fragile miraculous microcosmos of
cells and changeable protein molecules which we call the
living organism.

The author of this book has been under a real threat of
extinction for eleven years. He was condemned to die not
only by the natural forces, which eventually bring an end
to the life of each of us, but by an added large force of
common public emotion (indignation) and thought (law) because he had at one point threatened the life of another
human being.

Rarely are books written by criminals under prolonged
threat of extermination, except the diaries of political
rebels or the last statements and letters of those condemned
to die in military conflict.

It is not my function as a psychiatrist to give a psychiatric
diagnosis of the state of mind of the author, whom I have
never met. My own thoughts about death have been deeply
influenced by writers like Schopenhauer, who as a philosopher, and Thomas Mann, who as a poet, have taught me to
see death with equanimity if not with detachment. "As long
as we are, death is not. When we are gone, our thoughts
and memory and emotions are not; therefore there is no

connection between life and death." We will never know or experience the moment of our extinction, no matter how much we fear it before it arrives.

Nietzsche went even further. He said: "Of our death we are certain. Why should we not be cheerful?"

In a brilliant after-dinner lecture at the Harvard Club in Boston, I recently heard the scientist, philosopher and poet Warren S. McCulloch say that death comes to an organism when there are no further possibilities to put its built-in capacities for adaptation to a good use.

The end of Caryl Chessman's life, which has caused so many people to think about threats of violent death and retaliation by capital punishment, is discussed here more as a philosophical problem than a moral one. To be for or against capital punishment is a question on the same psychiatric level as whether we are for war or peace; whether our rational minds permit us to allow violent death to be brought about by us and our fellow men, or whether we can resist the temptation to become so utterly and definitely violent.

The author of this book sees the hero of his story as a killer, a man who cannot refrain from maximal violence, and he explains that the forces of society around him have made him that way; in other words he has lost his ability and his willingness to control his destructive impulses when he is angry, or when an opportunity for killing arises. He indicates that, if society makes us furious enough, or exposes us to enough cruelty, we may become killers.

No one has ever measured how much torture and cruelty a growing child must be exposed to in order to convert it into a mad killer. Certain organisms can stand a lot of punishment over a long time before they become antisocial, while others under the same stress break early. What baffles me is the fact that Caryl Chessman has managed to stir people up to such an extent; that many people left the normal middle field of neutrals and chose to move into either the violently indignant group which is for capital punishment, or the equally vociferous and emotional group which exclaims against capital punishment as a social sin and crime equal to the ones it seeks to avenge.

We psychiatrists think often in terms of unconscious (irrational) forces which steer our mind into various types of behavior. Which unconscious motives make us choose so emphatically for or against death by capital punishment? Those who believe in the primary goodness of man—the

vi

modern humanists among whom belong Thomas Mann and the present Pope—are powerfully motivated to believe that delaying violent action, holding and restraining the violent criminal without physically injuring him, leads to a better world because it gives the primary good in man a chance to develop further, rather than cutting him off from the world. These humanists must have experienced some good in their own young years which made them believe in the value of restraint and self-discipline. The other faction of our people, those who believe that criminal violence should be punished by death, have in their own lives experienced the consequences of hate and cruelty; they have learned to identify with the victims of violence and they wish vehemently to protect our community from aggression, not only from other external criminals, but also from the violence in their own hearts. Those who feel the need for capital punishment as a deterrent want not only to hold a threat over their aggressive fellow men, but also want to protect themselves from the possible temptation to break through their own capacity for reason and restraint, and commit major violence. It can be argued that there is nothing "morally" wrong with capital punishment. But it is an admission of our own inner weakness; in our need to protect ourselves, we "realistically" assume that sharp threats and acute danger of death are necessary to ward off man's sadistic impulses.

I do not know whether Caryl Chessman as a man has any merits. I cannot say anything more than this: he stirred us all to think about the violence in our own hearts, and that makes his impact on our society important.

Chapter One

THERE WAS A FAMINE in local sports news, one of those dead periods that crop up.

Borden, our aging and irascible little dynamo of a sports editor, sent for me. When I barged into the cluttered cubicle he called his office, he was restlessly pacing the floor, a green eyeshade cocked on his bald head.

"Evans," I was told brusquely, without preliminaries, "your column's getting anemic. Hell, man, it's practically old-maidish!"

I winced. But you didn't argue with Borden, the little man who could outshout Stentor. You heard him out. That way you saved a lot of wear and tear on your ears.

Borden continued, "Get off the seat of your pants and go out and dig us up a story with sock and human interest; something that'll hit the reader between the eyes. It's out there, I know it."

Then came the punch line, some famous last words: "All you gotta do is find it." The little devil smiled benignly.

"Yeah," I said icily, "all I have to do is find it. *But where?*"

Borden pivoted around and shouted, "How should I know! That's your job."

Sure, that was my job.

And didn't I have two eyes, two ears, two legs? Didn't I have the prescient Borden's ironclad assurance a Big Story was out there somewhere in our sprawling, sports-starved metropolis just waiting for Charley Evans, columnist and feature writer, to break it? What more did I need, a ouija board? The logic was perfect and, from Borden's standpoint, devastating.

I shrugged, smiled bleakly, and exited. Muttering darkly to myself about pint-sized sports editors of the rock 'em-sock 'em school of journalism, I threw the cover over the ancient Underwood on which I banged out my daily column and weekly features. Borden was, in his own way, a fox. He

1

knew I'd produce if I could. With him I shared a fierce pride in the fact that the sports section of our paper, the *Reporter-Times*, was regarded as one of the best in the country. Together we had built it up from nothing.

The five-foot five-inch Borden, who never seemed to unwind, supplied the brash, aggressive drive, the bristling, hunch-playing dynamism, while, I liked to think, I contributed the counterbalance needed to keep the roof from blowing off, as well as a sports column that was syndicated from coast to coast and weekly sports features which had boosted circulation impressively.

Now we were on a spot. We had a reputation to live up to and some really hot competition from a competing daily—the *Rag*, Bordon called it—which, under new ownership, had decided to take us on. A couple of months ago its new editor and publisher, after importing talent from all over the country, had announced that his paper would put out afternoon as well as morning editions, "with special emphasis on sports news." The fight was on. . . .

Borden stood at the door of his office and watched me, gimlet-eyed, as I sharpened a couple of pencil stubs and clapped on my hat.

Then I took a walk.

That was how it began.

Borden's words kept rattling around in my head—"a story with sock." Sock and human interest. To me, after cooling off in the brisk autumn air, those words added up literally to boxing. So I played a hunch, figuring my harassed, megaphone-mouthed boss held no corner on the crystal ball market. . . .

A few minutes later I was standing with Mike McGuire over in a corner of Larson's Gym, talking and watching Mike's boy, Angelo (the Angel) Marino, a half-Italian, half-Irish lad, going through his paces in the ring. A handsome—for a pug almost too handsome—twenty-three-year-old, the Angel was a sharp, scientific boxer, a real cutey, but no posturing Fancy Dan. No cream puff gladiator. At the moment he was displaying his wares to a rugged, free-swinging youngster his own age. And Mike was rhapsodizing about his boy, as managers will, assuring me that he would be the next light heavy champion of the world.

"Maybe," I said noncommittally, fishing for a lead, an

2

angle, "maybe not. You know how it goes, Mike. You can never be sure."

Mike wasn't buying any pessimism. "No maybes about it, Charley," he insisted, and he had his reasons catalogued and ready. "I'm bringing my Angel-boy along like they're supposed to be brought. Slow and sure. And he's got everything, Charley—savvy, guts, and a punch in either mitt. He's a natural. But, hell, you got eyes. You can see that for yourself."

Mike's enthusiasm, I knew, was composed of nine parts desperation. What he was telling me *had* to be right. He didn't dare face the possibility it wasn't, for Mike was a guy with a dream.

I'd known the grizzled, lovable old Irishman for more years then I cared to remember—way back almost three decades earlier, when I'd been a wide-eyed cub reporter and Roughhouse Mike McGuire had been Fistiana's brightest star, the most colorful light heavy in the country. In an overweight, nontitle match, Mike had easily kayoed the division's titleholder. It was then that he began to be called the uncrowned champ, and the next three 175-pounders to wear the crown would have no part of him. Undismayed, Mike finally had forced the signing of a title fight by barnstorming the country and eliminating every logical contender in sight.

At last, it had seemed, he was not to be denied. Then, two days before he was to have fought for the title, a drunken driver had crashed head on into the car in which he had been riding. In a coma for more than a week, he finally regained consciousness; the medics regarded his survival as a miracle. They had put a plate in his head and an end to his ring career. I'd scored a beat by being the first reporter to interview him after he regained consciousness. That interview had marked the beginning of a lifelong friendship and my own career as a sports writer. The accident had occurred in our city; it was here Roughhouse Mike McGuire made his home.

Mike never talked about what that plate meant and did to him, but I knew. Everyone in the fight game knew. We knew when he turned down a dozen lucrative business offers and, on a shoestring, began training and then managing fighters, either light heavies or young middleweights who would grow into that division. He was trying to transfer his dream to one of them, determined to win that light heavyweight title by proxy. But so far Fate had cold-decked him, seven times in a row. His fighters always started out great guns; under his expert tutelage, they fought their way to or near the No. 1 contending spot; then something happened. Accidents, the wrong kind of female, brittle hands, a swollen head. Something.

Now people along fighters' row were saying that Mike was jinxed and that he jinxed the boys he trained and managed. Even Mike had halfway come to believe this. If he failed with Angelo, he was through, washed up. He knew it.

So the question framed itself: Would he fail?

I wondered. As a friend, I hoped not, I hoped like hell not, but as a newspaperman on the prowl for copy I was obliged to be hardheadedly objective. It was true, the Angel had everything Mike claimed: youth and heart, punch, skill, a genuine love of combat. He had an impressive record as an amateur. He'd won all of his twenty-odd pro fights—but only two by a knockout. And those two kayos, in my opinion, had been flukes. That was the rub.

In the ring, Angelo was an artist, not a killer. A too-civilized young man in a primitive, punishing business, he was reluctant to bomb an opponent insensible. That was why I didn't figure him as championship material—not for a while at least. Borden might have called my column anemic and old-maidish, but I was still old-fashioned enough to believe that a fighter had to have that savage killer instinct to be a champion. And I was convinced that my reasons were practical, not romantic. . . .

Mike had continued talking, oblivious of my silence. He'd been too busy feasting his eyes on the precision-boxing Angelo. I watched until the round was over. Then I happened to glance in the direction of the main entrance of the gym.

4

Chapter Two

THE KID WHO ENTERED was tall, perhaps six feet, perhaps a fraction under. He looked to be about twenty-five, twenty-six years old, and he had a pug's fist-battered, broken-nosed face that, at the moment, was masked and expressionless. He stood inside the door, sizing up the place, the people. Our eyes locked and he stared at me in insolent appraisal. Then, unhurriedly, he walked with a slight limp over to where Mike and I were standing.

I tried being friendly. "Looking for somebody?" I asked.

"Yeah, mister, I am," the kid acknowledged. "I'm looking for somebody to fight."

Mike chuckled good-humoredly at this novel conversational gambit. "You sure come to the right place, son."

The kid glared at Mike; his gray-green eyes were cold and humorless, flinty, the kind of eyes you expected to see behind a young hoodlum's gun or in a rogues' gallery.

"I'm not kidding, grandpa."

"Got anybody special in mind?" I queried, not sure whether I had a hot column for Borden or whether I should write the kid off as a member of that pitiful, punch-drunk fraternity who had begun the long, one-way trip down Queer Street.

"Only somebody that knows how," the kid told me.

Mike asked, "You mean you want to fight in the ring?"

"Yeah," the kid said, his voice heavy with sarcasm, "I mean in the ring."

"Well, now, sonny, I think maybe we can accommodate you," Mike replied. His glance flicked from the kid to the Angel and back. "Had any experience?"

"Enough to beat anybody in this crum joint," was the flat reply.

"H'mm," Mike said, his eyes twinkling. Tough youngsters with gall amused him. "I don't think I caught the name you fight under."

5

"I don't fight under a name, grandpa. I just fight."

I knew that Mike was unorthodox enough to put a complete stranger in against Angelo. Borden or no Borden, I didn't like it, but I also knew it would be futile to try to do anything about it except ask a question or two.

"How much experience did you say you'd had, lad?"

"I said enough."

"Enough to beat the next light heavy champ?" Mike wanted to know.

The kid was plainly fed up with the questions. "Why don't you try me and find out?"

This was bait Mike couldn't resist. "Okay, son, if that's the way you want it."

Mike showed the kid to the dressing room while I walked over and spoke to Angelo, who had been shadowboxing around the ring after finishing his workout with his sparring partner.

"Feel like going another few rounds, Angelo?"

Angelo grinned. "Sure, Mr. Evans, if Mike wants me to."

"I think he does," I said, and explained the setup.

Angelo was a steady, easygoing youngster, in or out of the ring, and he had a sense of humor. "You have to promise me one thing, Mr. Evans," he said. "You have to promise that you won't let this double-tough character hurt me."

"I think you know how to take care of yourself, Angelo," I said, laughing.

The Angel's grin broadened; his dark eyes sparkled. "Thanks, Mr. Evans. I'll do my best."

Presently, following Mike, the kid emerged from the dressing room. Stripped down to an old pair of trunks and boxing shoes, he wasn't much of a physical specimen. Neither was he the ninety-eight-pound-weakling type. Just thin, without much muscle definition. But he had good shoulders and that meant he probably could hit. When he climbed between the ropes I saw the ugly, disfiguring scars on his chest, back, and legs—and I felt suddenly uneasy, vaguely worried.

Mike took over as third man in the ring. The kid refused a mouthpiece. He objected when Mike started to slip a pair of sixteen-ounce gloves over his wrapped hands.

"You can't do no fighting in those pillows, grandpa."

"Look, son," Mike said patiently, "if you're as hell-fire ferocious with your dukes as you say, then I got to give my boy a little protection, don't I?"

The kid shot a contemptuous look at the smiling, handsome Angelo. "Looks like maybe you should do his fighting too," he sneered.

Angelo's face crimsoned. He jerked off his headgear. Mike muttered an oath. They compromised for ten-ounce gloves, which the kid accepted reluctantly. He'd wanted sixes or eights.

Spectators, hangers-on, trainers, managers, and other fighters had got wind of what was coming off. By the time Mike had laced the gloves on the kid and spoken a few words of instruction to him and Angelo, everyone in the place was crowded around the ring, expecting either some two-fisted, whirlwind action or some comic relief.

"Boys," Mike announced, "I want to introduce you to the kid. He came here looking for a fight. Don't ask me why. He tells me he can whip anybody in this place, and maybe he can. Anyway, the point is, since he came here itching for a scrap and we are accommodating folks hereabouts, my Angelo has generously agreed to go two or three rounds with him. I——"

The kid cut in. "Whenever you get through beating your gums, grandpa, I'm ready to fight."

Mike flushed, then looked sad. Angelo was doing a slow burn. Those clustered around the ring booed and jeered.

"Give this big mouth a boxing lesson, Angelo!" somebody shouted.

"Yeah, teach him some manners!"

"Find out if he's as rough with his dukes as he is with his mouth!"

Mike held up a hand for silence. Then he nodded to Blinky, the timekeeper.

The bell rang.

The kid came out of his corner in a half crouch, carrying his gloves awkwardly in front of him, waist high. Experimentally, Angelo jabbed twice with his left. The kid shuffled forward, making no effort to counter. Angelo feinted, stepped in and snapped the kid's head back with a whistling uppercut. The kid didn't appear fazed by the punch. But he was still doing his fighting with his mouth. In a low voice he profanely derided Angelo and his ability.

Angered, Angelo set himself, jabbed, double-hooked to the head, then crossed explosively with his right. That should have ended it, before the kid had thrown punch one. Angelo stepped back.

But the kid didn't go down. He blinked, rocked on his

7

heels, shook his head, and smiled at Angelo in a way that made my flesh crawl. I was worried now in earnest. At worst the kid was a spoil-fighter, one of that maddening, dangerous breed who made even champions look bad with their unorthodox, deceptively clumsy styles and their incredible ability to take a beating. For Angelo's and Mike's sake, I hated to think about what the kid might be at best.

Angelo fired another right hand. The kid walked into it disdainfully, shook it off. "Is that the best you got to offer?" he mocked.

"I'm not in the habit of belting guys with their guard down, friend," Angelo said through his mouthpiece, forcing a calm into his voice I knew he didn't feel. "You've been doing a lot of talking about fighting. Now let's see you do some!"

"Don't worry about me, pretty face. Have your fun while you got a chance. Punks like you are my specialty."

"Why, you . . ."

"Yeah?"

"Nothing."

His fighter's confidence severely shaken, his male pride cut to the quick, the Angel opened up then. He'd teach this brash, skinny, big-mouthed kid a lesson! He looked as disciplinedly savage as any fighter I'd ever watched. Probably for the first time in his ring career, he had in front of him not an opponent to be outpointed, but an enemy to be blasted to the canvas without mercy.

Without letup, Angelo rocked, jarred, and bombed the kid for the remainder of the round, throwing combinations and hard right hands until he grew arm-weary. The kid appeared to take terrifying pleasure in absorbing the punishment, in being a human, weirdly smiling punching bag. Angelo had opened a cut over the kid's left eye. The kid's face soon was smeared with blood. A succession of blows whipped to the body turned the kid's chest and stomach into one angry red welt. But when the round ended the kid was still firmly on his feet.

At the bell the only sound was Angelo's labored breathing. The rest of us were too stunned to say anything. If nothing else, the kid had proved he could take it. Gently, Mike tried to convince the kid he'd had enough.

"What the hell do you mean, had enough!" the kid exploded. "I just wanted to let you jokers see for yourselves that this pretty-faced punk of yours is a pure phony. He can't

8

box apples." The derision was obscene. "Besides," the kid snarled, "I ain't had my turn yet. Is that what you're scared of, grandpa? You afraid I might run this phony champ of yours out of the ring?"

"Let it go, Mike," Angelo said grimly.

Mike did, reluctantly. He signaled Blinky.

Angelo left his corner determined to put the kid away fast. In his mind, he had to. That was obvious. More than his pride was at stake now, more than his reputation as a fighter. Somehow, in some evil way, Angelo Marino, the man, had been placed on trial.

Unwisely Angelo threw aside caution; he elected to wade in and slug—and promptly ran into trouble. He found himself crowded, tricked, goaded. Defensively, amazingly, the kid had come to life. With mounting desperation, Angelo threw leather the entire round. His punches either went wild or were smothered. The kid taunted Angelo, mocked him, feinted him out of position, spun him into the ropes, bulled him across the ring, grinning hideously all the time like some blood-smeared gargoyle.

The round finally ended. The kid hadn't yet thrown a solid punch, though he'd slapped and cuffed Angelo a few times. There was no talk now of stopping it. Mike didn't dare. If he did, the word would get around, the rumors. "Didja hear the latest?" they'd say. "No? Well, it seems that some tough-talking kid that nobody's ever heard of was about to give Angelo Marino the business when McGuire jumps in and stops it." The story would get better every time it was told.

Mike looked at me helplessly, a stricken friend with a viciously shattered dream. I was sick. Angelo's words, spoken with an easy jocularity only minutes ago, rang in my ears: "You have to promise that you won't let this double-tough character hurt me." Now, too late, I realized that physical courage and physical skill, even physical violence, were no defense against the sort of incarnate evil that confronted Angelo. I cursed softly.

The kid was leering at all of us, that terrible smile frozen on his blood-smeared face. We held our breath, knowing without any doubt what was coming, powerless to stop it, unable even to look away, so hypnotic was the kid's diabolic hold on us. Already victory belonged to the kid. It was complete, and all wrong.

Blinky, resentfully sensing what the rest of us did, stalled

9

for an extra fifteen or twenty seconds before banging the bell for round three.

Angelo and the kid met in the center of the ring. "Now, pretty face," the kid jeered, "I'm going to beat your god-damned brains out—if you got any."

The kid proceeded to do just that, almost literally. He did what he had let Angelo do to him in the first round, yet with far more deadly, sadistic efficiency. He cut, hammered, and slashed. A crunching right hand drove the Angel across the ring. Twice he had the reeling, glassy-eyed Angelo set up for the kill. Each time, deliberately, contemptuously, he let him get away. Finally the humiliation proved too much for Angelo. He dropped his guard, stumbled to face the kid.

"Finish it! Damn you, finish it!"

The kid and Angelo stood facing each other for four or five seconds, creating a terrible tableau. Then the kid said, "All right, pretty face, here it comes!"

Angelo made no effort to get out of the way. The kid took his time. His right hand, with a lot of leverage behind it, smashed into Angelo's face. Angelo spun and dropped, his head striking the canvas with a dull thud. The kid didn't bother to look. He turned to Mike.

"Thanks for the workout, grandpa. I'll be back again one of these days."

I watched the kid, limping slightly, disappear into the dressing room. Then, with the others, I turned my attention to Angelo. It was a good five minutes before he regained consciousness. Mike was frantic. He rushed Angelo to the hospital. I tried to find the kid then but he'd gone, vanished.

Chapter Three

THE STORY, carrying my by-line and banged out at top speed on my ancient Underwood while Borden excitedly hovered and jumped about, shouting at me, firing questions, and snatching the sheets from the typewriter as I completed them, made the late afternoon and night editions. I headed it "The Kid Was a Killer," and Borden played it up, big, giving it the banner treatment. He even wangled a bold page one headline: MYSTERY FIGHTER HOSPITALIZES MARINO. *See Sports.*

In the body of the story, against the background of an old fighter's bright dream, I'd shot the works, graphically detailing the improbable events, the sneering words, and the violent action at Larson's Gym earlier in the day. I'd begun and ended with a question: "Is Mike McGuire jinxed?"

Borden was vocally in his glory. I wasn't. He had his real-life, slam-bang story with sock and human interest, even mystery, and a made-to-order villain; one that, with the impact of a sledge hammer, "hit the reader between the eyes," put our department back in the center of the universe—and sold newspapers. A magic combination.

That was what Borden had.

I had a guilty conscience.

With my writing chore out of the way, the deadline met, the pressure off, depression set in. I was, I told myself, in a sorry business. Irrationally, I began to feel a bitter, personal responsibility for the kid. I tried to suppress the feeling, to shove it out of my mind, to rationalize it away. But it wouldn't go. Like a poisonous fog, it penetrated my newspaperman's cynicism, permeating the thinking part of me, framing an indictment that really didn't make sense. At least not logical, two-and-two-makes-four sense. But neither did what had happened make that kind of sense. That was why, mentally, I found myself running in circles. . . .

11

Borden had been turning the city upside down trying to find the kid. He'd got nowhere. Fast. I heard him bellow into his office phone and looked up to see him come storming across the office, the green eyeshade dangerously askew on his round bald head.

Thirty feet from my desk he shouted: "Dammit, Evans, a *good* reporter wouldn't've let that kid get away!"

I shrugged. "I missed the boat."

"Well," Borden fumed, his indignation rising with his blood pressure at my lack of penitence, "you're not going to catch it sitting here on your skinny behind, twiddling your thumbs."

"Meaning now you want me to play detective?"

That was the idea. What really gave Borden the horrors, of course, was the possibility, however remote, that "The Rag" would locate the kid, steal most of Borden's headlined thunder and give him the loud hee-haw. Borden at least was consistent. First, last, and always he could be depended upon to be looking out for Borden.

"Sam Catchem at your service," I said sarcastically, pushing myself up out of my chair and bowing slightly from the waist.

Looking for the kid was as good an excuse as any to get away from the office and myself for a while, to substitute motion for reflection. *Mine not to reason why,* I thought sardonically.

For almost five hours I drove around, legged it, quizzed people, looked in likely and unlikely places, and made at least two dozen phone calls. In the end I drew a blank. I'd expected to all along. And if I found the kid, I asked myself, what then? Probably I'd get a quick punch in the nose (or a swift kick in the backside, depending upon the target then presenting itself) for sticking that reportorial organ into his private life.

If the kid was one of those dime-a-dozen exhibitionistic characters with a barroom brawler's pea-brained mentality, say, a real-life Pal Smirch, he'd have identified himself, stuck around, mugged for our photographers and eaten up the publicity. Hell, that was obvious; it had been from the beginning. And I was tired of playing any more games with myself or Borden or anybody. So I phoned Borden and said flatly I was positive the kid didn't intend to let himself be found. I told him why.

12

"You don't think 'The Rag' will be able to run him down?" Borden asked.

"No. And if some bright boy on it should, I'll give you a double-your-money-back guarantee that it'll have a hospitalized reporter to keep Angelo company and no story."

Borden chuckled evilly. He got bighearted. I could take the rest of the night off.

"You're too good to me," I said, and hung up.

It was a few minutes past midnight. I thought about Mike; the poor guy was unquestionably going through hell. I headed my coupé for Clancy's Bar & Grill, a favorite hangout of those connected with the fight game, certain I'd find Mike there if he'd left the hospital. It turned out he had.

As soon as I entered I spotted him sitting alone at a booth in a far corner, away from the crowd, the sports. He had our night final laid out on the table in front of him and was staring gloomily at Borden's bold-faced spread and my by-line. His big shoulders sagged; the life had gone out of him. I slid in opposite him and ordered a bottle of beer. We nodded to each other.

"How's Angelo, Mike?"

Mike sighed. "The doc tells me he's got a mild concussion besides those bad cuts and a busted nose. Doc says he'll be good as new in a couple of months. But I just got through having a long talk with him, Charley; they finally ran me out. That beating he took did the worst damage on the inside, where it doesn't show but where it hurts most. He's already talking about hanging 'em up. You know what that means."

"Yeah, Mike, I know. I only wish there was something I could do. Believe me, this"—I tapped the paper—"was the toughest story I ever had to write. The weirdest part is that we haven't been able to find a trace of the kid."

The waiter brought my beer and we sat for a while in silence. After thirty years of pursuing a dream, this for Mike was one blow too many. It was something he couldn't shrug or laugh off. The bitterness was welling up in him. Soon it came spilling out in a rush of words.

"My God, Charley, I *must* be jinxed! How else can you explain it? This crazy-mean kid walks in, insults everybody in the place, beats my boy half to death, thanks me, and walks out like nothing has happened. And I let it happen, Charley! I was the fat, dumb, and happy fool who let it happen!"

13

"It wasn't your fault, Mike," I insisted. "You had no way of knowing." I talked fast and earnestly, even trying to sell Mike on the idea that, in some inexplicable way, it was Borden's and my fault, because we were the ones who had benefited, but Mike wouldn't listen. He kept blaming himself, and he confided that the more he thought about it, the less he could believe that the kid had been human.

"I know what you mean, Mike. Remember, I was there too."

Perhaps it wasn't so much a case of knowing as it was one of feeling. It was as though some incarnate fiend from the Pit, just for the sheer, sadistic hell of it, had walked in and done this to Mike and Angelo. It was that cruelly senseless, on the surface at least.

And Borden—damn him!—was happy.

Mike asked the question I'd been dreading: "What do we do now, Charley? Now that the damage is done?"

How did you put Humpty Dumpty back together again?

"We `. . . well, we figure something out. We convince Angelo he mustn't quit. We . . ."

What? What more? I didn't know. I subsided helplessly.

Mike and I sat there for several minutes, lost in brooding thought. The leering, blood-smeared face of the kid danced in front of our eyes. I damned that cold-eyed face a hundred times—and wondered when I would see it again and what I would do when I did.

Thanks for the workout, grandpa, the kid had said. *I'll be back again one of these days. . . .*

Chapter Four

I WAS AT THE OFFICE the next morning early, with a fresh sheet of paper fed into my old typewriter. I had a column to get out. This one was more than singing for my supper.

"Yesterday at Larson's Gym," I began, pecking out the words with two fingers, "evil had its day. And this writer for one doesn't like it."

I didn't like sadism.

Or physical violence for its own sake.

Or ugly mean characters like the kid who mocked what, to my mind, was right and decent.

I said so, banging the typewriter keys emphatically in the process. I reported my talk with Mike, repeated his question: "What do we do now, Charley? Now that the damage is done?"

"What has happened to these two people," I went on, leaving the question hanging for a paragraph, "to this old fighter and to this young fighter, is not in essence different from what is happening in the world today. We—you and I, the normal people—are being challenged, not by an opponent who seeks to meet us on honorable terms, in a spirit of 'may the best man win,' but by an Enemy who is implacably dedicated to destroying or enslaving us entirely. To him sportsmanship, as we know it, is a term of utmost contempt. He refuses to play by the rules. He recognizes no law but the law of the jungle, the law of claw and cunning and fang. What better opportunity will we ever have than right now, in the case of Mike McGuire and Angelo Marino, to meet this challenge and . . ."

I stopped typing, stared at the paragraph. "Oh, hell," I thought aloud, "this isn't what I'm really trying to say." The words looked too stilted, too pretentious. I wasn't the editorializer; Borden was. With a rip, out came the sheet of paper; in went a new one. I tried it again.

What do we do now, Charley?

15

"We give these two friends a vote of confidence," I wrote. "We let them know we're standing solidly behind them. And we don't glamorize this mean and mysterious youngster, this tough no-good who will get his before it's over. His kind never wind up a winner in the end. The real winners are good, decent people like Mike McGuire and Angelo Marino."

That was a little better. I made some minor penciled corrections and then gave the typed column to a copy boy. Now that I'd unburdened myself, a bit bravely perhaps, I felt better, but not much. I'd become too personally and emotionally involved. I'd never be satisfied until—well, until what? Until Angelo was champion? Until Mike saw a thirty-year dream come true? That was part of it, a big part. But it also went deeper than that. And it was difficult to put nicely into words. I was certain only that an evil had entered our lives, upsetting their balance, contaminating them. Somehow, decisively, we had to purge ourselves of this contamination.

But how? Dammit, *how*?

I didn't know—yet. There had to be a way.

I stared at the phone on my desk. Ten, twenty, thirty seconds passed. A minute. The phone didn't ring, but suddenly a bell in my mind did. Some weeks ago I'd done a column—"The Psychology of the Athlete," I'd called it—following a lengthy and provocative interview with one of our city's younger psychiatrists, Dr. Thomas Layton, himself no stranger to sports. Was it possible that the doctor held the key? It unquestionably was possible. Even probable.

Fifteen years before, as a long-legged, ironhearted college boy, Tom Layton had been burning up the country's tracks and rewriting the record books. World War II took him from college and put him in the cockpit of a fighter plane. In 1943, over occupied France, he was struck by flak. Half-conscious and half-blinded, his left leg almost shot away below the knee, he coaxed his battered plane back to England and crash-landed. The doctors there amputated immediately. Later plastic surgeons repaired the damage to his face. His vision was permanently impaired.

For Tom Layton the war was over. He was taught to walk with an artificial limb, sent back to the States and honorably discharged. He returned to college, graduated with honors, went to medical school, served his internship, and then, after further intensive study and training at a large clinic in the Midwest, became a psychiatrist.

Meanwhile his passionate interest in sports hadn't waned. Where before he had brought to them an exceptionally fast pair of legs, he now contributed a dedicated, professionally trained mind. This was the tall young man who had supplied the stimulating information for my column.

Borden had signified his reaction to the piece by holding his nose—until batches of letters from our readers began to pour in complimenting me on it and asking for more. Since he had come to regard himself as the Grand Panjandrum of sports in our city, this positive response had visibly unsettled the opinionated little villain. To rebuke my heresy and reassert his own authority, he'd done a scorching diatribe, thinly disguised as an editorial, inviting all psychiatrists to take themselves and their couches elsewhere. In the course of his harangue he'd professed outrage at "the sinister prospect of having the minds of our fine young athletes picked by some bloodless old geezer with a beard." He'd made it sound positively indecent.

Well, figuratively speaking, Borden could drop dead; in a follow-up column, while not naming him, I virtually had invited him to do just that. His prattle, his fatuous thrust at "Freudian eggheads," hadn't impressed me, the doctor—or very many readers. But the word storm it had kicked up, and our apparent feud, had been good for circulation and appeared to have satisfied Borden who then, with the immoderate enthusiasm of a small-beer Don Quixote with ants in his mental and emotional pants, had gone on to tilt furiously with other windmills.

Characteristically, of course, Borden had blithely chosen to ignore the point, like a man who grows readers in his journalistic garden and whose words are gratuitous smudge pots used to prevent the readers' exposure to too many facts, to too much truth. The overlooked point was this:

You—you personally and you editorially—were gravely mistaken if you thought you would rob any sport of its inherent vitality, its impassionate glamor, its attraction, its thrills by grasping its dynamics and the psychodynamics of both participant and spectator. On the contrary, you would breathe pulsing new life into it. Moreover, you couldn't nicely isolate sports from life and daily living, from the larger realities of each, their triumphs and defeats, their rewards and punishments. They were inseparable, and rightly

17

so, the shrill opinion of one very hardheaded and affectedly hardboiled sports editor notwithstanding.

Implicitly, sports spelled competition (when you won, another or others lost), and competition, given the right milieu and the right incentives, the right stimuli, was a healthy form of conflict. An obvious and elementary proposition? Granted. As obvious and elementary—and yet as complex and profound, as charged with deductive significance—as life and death.

It was here that you reached the very heart of the matter. Whether it was conflict between nations, groups, or individuals, the lesson to be learned was to handle it creatively. Failure to do so, a refusal to learn the lesson in this age of the stockpiled Hell-bomb, the armed, ideological camp, and the deceptively simple equation $e = mc^2$, could mean extinction of the human race. Brave words were scarcely a match for deadly radiation.

This Dr. Thomas Layton had emphasized to me. He had concerned himself sympathetically and empathetically with the non-winner and the near winner as well as with the winner, the guy who always was out in front. A lost leg and injured vision had taken him from one race and put him in another: "The race," as he put it, "to promote man's understanding of man before mankind incinerates itself." In this context, the distance between the front pages and the sports pages was slight indeed. A step and you were there. . . .

I snatched up the phone and dialed this young psychiatrist's number. A receptionist answered. I asked for and was given the doctor. He sounded genuinely pleased to hear from me again. I got right down to cases.

"Doctor, I've run into a problem. It's too big for me. I need help."

Was the problem personal or professional? I was asked. I thought about this a moment. Actually, which was it?

"Both."

"And you think I can help?"

"I do, definitely."

"I tell you what. I'll be in my office for another hour or so. Why don't you drop over and we can discuss it."

"Thanks, I will." I cradled the phone.

The mercurial Borden, like a manic-depressive on the upswing, was lapping the office, taking his bow. He had a scoop wrapped up, tied with pink ribbon. (The kid appeared safely

18

beyond the reach of "The Rag.") Once more the world was a rosy place; again, fittingly of course, it had rewarded his unique genius. He stopped at my desk, waving yesterday's sports section and the proofs of my day's column at me.

"How about it, Charley"—it was "Charley" now—"can I smell an exclusive a mile off or can't I?" he asked smugly.

I reached out and took both the sports section and the proofs. "Borden," I said dryly, getting to my feet, "you're in a class all by yourself. Now, if you'll excuse me . . ."

Borden didn't appreciate my needle or the brush-off, and he had a suspicious mind. His eyebrows drew together in a storm-warning frown. "You got a new lead on this kid you haven't told *me* about, Charley? You holding out maybe?"

The temptation was too great to resist. "No, Borden; nothing like that." I paused. I smiled. Everybody in the office was listening. "The truth of the matter is, I got an appointment with a psychiatrist!"

"Touché!" somebody said *sotto voce,* and the place exploded with gusts of laughter.

For a moment it appeared as though Borden, too, would explode. He resembled a character in one of those old slapstick comedies who had just had a custard pie unlovingly shoved in his face. His mouth was working furiously, fish-out-of-water fashion, but the words were coming out crosswise and unintelligibly. He seemed to be saying "Glob, glob, glob!" which I knew wasn't what he was thinking. From past performance I also knew this vocal disability was anything but permanent.

Grinning, I got out of there fast, before my "glob-globbing" and volatile little boss recovered his voice and blew me out.

19

Chapter Five

DR. THOMAS LAYTON sat on the edge of his highly polished, glass-covered desk, sucking on an unlit pipe, and listened attentively to what I had to say. Impressively tall and clean-shaven, in his mid-thirties, his sandy hair crew cut, he was the antithesis of Borden's vulgar caricature of a psychiatrist —a brain-picking "bloodless old geezer with a beard." True, the horn-rimmed, thick-lensed glasses he wore gave his young-old face an owlish, bookish appearance; yet there was nothing remote about him, no air of condescending superiority or musty aloofness. His friendliness, his warm, lively interest in people as human beings, was genuine, unaffected. He was easy to talk to.

I began at the beginning, with Borden and his *ipse dixit* brand of clairvoyance. Continuing, I recounted how, on a hunch, I'd gone to Larson's Gym to see Mike. Then I handed him the sports section of our yesterday's paper.

"You'll find the rest of the story there."

The doctor read my by-lined account. Slowly and thought-fully he reread it. At length he commented: "It appears, ironically, that your formidable Mr. Borden's self-serving omniscience has been put to the test and found not want-ing."

"That's the hell of it," I said. "Now, well . . . here, read these." I handed him the proofs of my day's column.

The doctor read them and frowned, tapping his pipe against his teeth, thinking, ingesting what I'd written. After a moment he looked up.

I plunged. "I know it doesn't make sense doctor, but I can't shake the feeling that Borden and I, in our need, con-jured this murderous kid up from hell. No, I don't mean literally, of course. Or maybe I do."

I hesitated.

"Yes, go on."

I proceeded then to explain my baffled anger, my unease,

20

a nagging conscience, the best way I could: If Borden hadn't needled me about the low iron content of my column, if he hadn't rousted me into looking for a story, and if I hadn't played a hunch and gone to see Mike, then *this*—this travesty, this grotesque fiasco—would never have occurred. Mike's dream still would be intact, and Angelo's face and his pride and his manhood. In a pedestrian way, without the intrusion of any savage and senseless melodrama, these two friends still would be campaigning for the light heavy title. There would be no complications, at least no extraordinary, headline-making ones with diabolically superhuman implications and, with Borden involved, coarsely humorous connotations—and no obscenely grinning, lethal-fisted kid.

The double-damned kid was a mocking riddle. To me, he personalized, symbolized a kind of vicious universal evil. He'd contemptuously flung down a challenge. He'd said, in effect, "All right, mister, I've had my fun. Now what're you going to do about it? Think it over, mister; think it over real good, because I'll be back one of these days and find out." If and when he returned, I had to be ready for him; ready to call his hand. I had to see him defeated utterly, the thing he stood for repudiated wholly.

"He'll be back," the doctor said. "I'm sure of it."

"Sure," I agreed, "he'll be back. He'll be back to have another laugh, to furnish Borden with another story, and—" I shrugged helplessly. Then the anger came. "Doctor," I said harshly, "that kid was a killer." He'd killed Mike's good dream; he might have killed Angelo. And, perversely, sickeningly, he'd enjoyed his evil handiwork.

"Why?"

Dr. Layton answered promptly with one softly articulated word:

"Hate."

He walked to a bookcase and selected a thick work on abnormal psychology, thumbing through it until he found the page he wanted.

"The kid, as you call him, Charley, is a dangerously sick young man."

"You mean he's some kind of maniac? That he's bugs, crazy?"

The doctor shook his head. "No, not crazy, Charley, sick; desperately sick, spiritually and psychologically."

"That's hard to swallow," I blurted out, caught off guard. It sounded too much like a whitewashing, an apology for

21

conduct that to my mind was indefensibly mean and wrong, downright evil. I said so, perhaps too sharply, even impertinently, unwilling to admit then that the kid could have any excuse, any justification for what he'd done and for being the sort of person he was.

"Besides, doctor," I added stiffly, "you don't know the kid. You've never even seen him. I have. So how can you . . .?"

Undismayed by my sudden incivility, Tom Layton said mildly, smiling, "Call me Tom, Charley, and remember that I'm on your side."

"I'm sorry, Tom," I said, chastened. "Forgive me for being a boor." I smiled feebly and added, "I guess I've been around Borden too long. After all, when I ran into a stone wall, it was I who came to *you* for help."

"And I want to help, to do all I can for you and young Angelo and Mike. Take my word for that. But I'd be neither helpful nor honest if I were uncritically to agree with you that, to put it crudely, the kid—I'll call him that too—is a rotten, no-good sonofabitch who deserves no better than to be run to earth, caged, cursed, and spat at. Such a course would hardly establish our virtue or moral superiority."

"You're right, of course."

It was one of those times when being right was considerably more difficult than being righteous.

"And you are equally right in saying that I don't know the kid personally, but I do know him as a clinical entity, and on that level I believe I can tell you a great deal that is relevant about him."

Dr. Tom Layton could and did.

"You see, Charley, in earlier centuries, and to some degree today, people would say the kid was possessed by a demon, an evil spirit, and hence that he was in league with the devil. Even you, a newspaperman, a realist trained to sort out fact from fiction, find yourself acutely disturbed by what appears to be an element of the metaphysical—or, to use your term, the diabolical—in these events. It's this element that, seemingly, supplies the events with explicable cohesion. Otherwise they would seem senseless and, by logical extension, so would our lives. Why? Because once we accept the premise flowing from them we're obliged to conclude that existence is ruled by force and chance and unreason. And that puts us back in the jungle. It leaves us Godless. It means we are going nowhere but to the grave. It makes our moral code a joke. Am I correct?"

22

He was. I said so.

This, falteringly, was what I had tried to say in my column. Words hadn't failed me; perception had. I had been groping blindly in the dark.

"Thus," the doctor continued, "you understandably find yourself involved, accountable. You've witnessed and, *a posteriori*, universalized the temporary triumph of what, to avoid semantic complications, we'll call an evil force. You're determined to see this force in this particular instance bested decisively. The problem that plagues you is, How?"

I nodded in agreement, not interrupting, hanging onto the words.

There was a trace of rue in the doctor's smile, a quirk of regret. The same problem, the doctor pointed out, had been baffling man—theologians, metaphysicians, thinkers of every kind and persuasion—from man's societal infancy. Or should it be said that man had been baffling himself with the problem?

"In either case, unfortunately, humanity's battle with evil has not been conspicuously successful, and we who study the mind today believe we know one of the reasons why. We're convinced that demon possession, if you elect to label it such, isn't a supernatural phenomenon, but a psychological one. A personality, as well as the physical machine itself, can become ill, can be injured, thrown out of balance, warped. Then, in some instances, hostility, hatred, and rebellion become its dominant traits; violence its tragic métier, and, paradoxically, peace its unconscious goal.

"But the ages, Charley, have blindly refused to recognize their responsibility to anyone so afflicted. In the past we've been content to damn and destroy, to punish, to cry for vengeance, to employ negative and destructive methods that are hopeless anachronisms."

Tom Layton paused to light his pipe. Having done so, his eyes bored into me almost hypnotically. "Let me add, Charley, that to recognize this and to acknowledge that a little humility is not a dangerous or subversive thing, isn't to blur the social, legal, and spiritual distinctions we make between right and wrong, good and evil. Rather, it's to sharpen them, to give them a workable meaning and a positive, creative validity. In short, Charley, I don't believe that ignorance, even righteous and pious ignorance, however well intentioned, is the best judge of evil; nor do I believe that it is a competent weapon to oppose evil."

23

My head had begun to whirl in trying to keep up. "I think I follow you so far, doctor . . . I mean Tom. You're telling me, gently, that it's wisest to understand before I righteously damn, and to reflect before I arbitrarily and grandly draw cosmic lines."

"Yes, Charley, that's what I'm trying to tell you. I'm also trying to tell you that I'm afraid the kid is under a sentence of death."

The words were like a clap of thunder.

"What?" I stammered. "How? I mean—"

Dr. Tom Layton explained quietly and matter-of-factly. He read from the book in his hand a section devoted to "Psychopathy: the Aggressive Psychopathic Personality." He made clear the meaning of the more technical terms. When I left his office I was sick at heart. I'd been blind, something of a righteous fool for all my professed humanity. Now, for the present, all I could do was wait—and hope.

And think . . . think . . .

Put under a microscope a philosophy of life that had been fifty-one years in forming. Revise it. Redefine the words on which it was built, recognize its imperfect abstractions, reconcile it with so much that was disparate and incongruous, tragic and comic.

Synthesize. Bring together.

Employ, not as a dramatic gesture, but as the fulfillment of a welcomed moral obligation, the power of a human mind to accomplish human good. Humbly and gratefully do this.

Act, finally. The time would come.

Act with certainty and conviction and faith.

Chapter Six

ANGELO'S UPCOMING SCRAP with the No. 2 contender was canceled. His own national rating was dropped from the No. 4 to the No. 10 spot. Sports pundits, especially those eager beavers on "The Rag," were ready to write him off as a flash in the pan.

"Your boy's not ready yet," Joe Fisch, our city's great-bellied, cigar-smoking boss promoter told Mike. "He can't be," Joe Fisch added bluntly, "not when he lets some green, unknown amateur give him the shellacking he did."

Mike flinched. "Joe," he said, "you think Angelo's through. But you're wrong."

Joe Fisch shrugged and shifted his cigar to the other side of his mouth. "I didn't say he was through, Irish. I just said he ain't ready for the big time now."

"But you'll give us a fight when I prove to you he's ready?" Mike asked hopefully.

"I'll give you a fight," the shrewd, unsentimental Fisch rejoined, "when *he* proves to me he's ready."

Out of the hospital and on the mend, Angelo was a tortured youngster, silent and unsmiling, unable to forget his humiliation. He wanted to call it quits but so far he'd made no final decision. What was holding him back, I knew, was his strong sense of loyalty to Mike and the rest of us who remained solidly behind him, scores of friends and hundreds of die-hard fans who'd written him encouraging letters as a result of my column. He didn't want to let us down, but he didn't ever want to climb between the ropes of a boxing ring again either. This dilemma had horns and either way he turned, the horns kept goring him, painfully reminding him.

"You need a rest and a change of scenery for a few weeks," Mike told him. "We won't even think about the future until you get back."

Angelo spent nearly a month at his parents' farm upstate.

25

When he returned Mike and I met him and drove him to Dr. Tom Layton's office. Tom Layton gave him a thorough physical and pronounced him in perfect condition.

"Angelo," the doctor said, "I'm a psychiatrist and I'm familiar with your history. I know you want to give up boxing. I know why. However, Mike and Charley didn't bring you here in the hope that I would be able to convince you to change your mind. That's a decision you must make yourself and I have no intention of trying to influence you one way or the other. But I want to tell you this: there is absolutely no valid reason why you shouldn't continue fighting."

"So we were wondering," Mike said diffidently, "if you'd be willing to work out at least one more time before you made up your mind."

"I will if you want me to, Mike," Angelo said. "But," he added tonelessly, "I don't think it will make any difference."

"You can never tell," I said. "It might make all the difference."

It could; and it meant at the very least that we were over one high hurdle. We got up to leave.

"Thanks, doctor," Mike said.

Tom Layton nodded. He offered Angelo his hand. "Good luck," he said.

I hung back for a moment.

"It's up to you now, Charley," Tom Layton told me. "Remember, he needs to be stung."

"Depend on me," I promised. "I'll see that he's stung but good."

Through my good offices "The Rag" was promptly furnished with an anonymous hot tip on our call on Tom Layton. Results were swift and edifying. Swallowing the bait with one greedy gulp, it cranked out for its sports final a nasty piece captioned: WHIPPED ANGEL SEES PSYCHIATRIST, with an accompanying cartoon in the corner of which was a familiar bald-headed figure wringing his hands.

"Here's something I think you ought to see," I told Borden, tossing him the paper.

Borden took one look and boiled over. Posthaste he turned out one of his famous "editorials," righteously blasting "The Rag" and stoutly defending the efficacy of psychiatric counseling! He concluded by flatly predicting that Angelo would be the next light heavy champ.

"I guess that ought to show those dunceheads!" Borden spluttered.

"It should," I conceded, marveling. To put it mildly, something he would never consider doing, my terrible-tempered little boss was a remarkable acrobat. Fire him up enough and an intellectual backflip through an emotional hoop was no feat at all. Presently, thanks to my own low cunning and his dazzling acrobatics, he had his neck stuck out a mile. The realization must have penetrated his hairless pate as he stood there in front of my desk and began to cool off, for a crafty look spread itself across his homely face.

He whispered confidentially, "You know, don't you, Charley, that I did that editorial just for you?"

"Borden," I said, "you're a real pal."

Now, if his prediction and his flipflop on psychiatry backfired on him, Borden had an out. He had a goat. Me. Good old Charley Evans. Mr. Fixit.

Well, I'd asked for it. . . .

I made it a point to be at the gym when Angelo showed up for his first workout. He came alone and changed into an old sweat shirt, sweat pants and boxing shoes. To warm up he skipped a little rope; nothing fancy, like the old days, just clop, clop, clop monotonously. Then, mechanically, he punched the light bag. Everybody in the place was watching him and making it more obvious by pretending not to. He couldn't fail to be aware of the covert scrutiny but he didn't appear self-conscious. He simply lacked animation, a pugilist's fire. He was remote, drawn into himself, almost an automaton.

"Ready for a little session in the ring?" Mike asked him.

"Yes," Angelo said, no expression on his tanned, handsome face.

Roughly paternal, trying to hide his anxiety, Mike laced the gloves on the Angel. He talked to him casually but firmly, as though this was just another, if important, workout, not the crossroads of a career.

Mike had picked Louie, an old pro and a workhorse, for Angelo's sparring partner. Louie wasn't too bright but he was tough and dependable. Waiting, he danced in his corner, shadowboxing and making snorting noises through his crooked nose.

Earlier I'd warned Mike: "No matter how you feel, don't tell Louie to take it easy. It wouldn't solve anything and Angelo'd never forgive you if you did."

Mike had agreed and Louie had been ordered not to

lighten up. I knew what a tough, painful decision this had been for Mike to make.

"Today we'll get right down to business," Mike said. "No pussyfooting."

Angelo nodded. All the nod said was that he understood.

"You feel all right?" Mike asked.

Angelo said yes, he felt all right.

"Good. Then I guess we're ready."

"I'm ready," Angelo said.

Mike waved to Blinky. The bell rang. Mike wanted Angelo to go for three three-minute rounds.

I stood at the base of the ring and watched, my fingers crossed. Louie meticulously followed instructions; snorting and grunting, he shot across the ring and went right to work. Instinctively Angelo began to defend himself. Louie kept crowding him. Ten seconds passed; twenty. A succession of stiff, jolting left jabs stung Angelo, awakened the fighter in him. Briefly he forgot the trauma, his conflict, his confusion. For half a minute he was a smooth, brilliantly coordinated boxing machine, magically alive and on the offensive. Then, during a good exchange, with Angelo beating Louie to the punch and whipping across a sizzling right hand, Louie grinned admiringly.

The grin did it.

Angelo froze. Louie fired and connected with his own right before he realized Angelo had stopped fighting.

"Jeez!" Louie exclaimed, befuddled. "Did I do something wrong?"

"It's all right, Louie," Angelo said.

Without another word, Angelo ducked between the ropes and walked quickly to the dressing room. Mike followed. So did I. Here it was, the showdown.

Mike tried to put it off. "Maybe you better rest for another week or two, Angelo," he said desperately. "Then you'll feel better."

The bitterness inside Angelo was etched on his face, and a harsh bitterness was in his voice. "Look, Mike, let's face it—now. There's no use in me trying to kid anybody, especially myself. Every time I get near a pair of boxing gloves I'll be thinking about that damned kid and what he did to me. It happened today when Louie grinned, and I knew it was going to happen. It's no good that way. I'm through."

"Well, son," Mike said slowly, "I guess I know how you feel, all right. But you proved today you still got plenty of

28

stuff left. It seems a shame to throw all that talent of yours away after we've spent five years developing it. And just on account of some big-mouthed kid beating you on a fluke."

"It wasn't a fluke, Mike. Everybody knows it wasn't. Besides, I'm not a fighter any more. I'm a joke, even to myself. They wouldn't give us a title fight now if I beat King Kong with one hand tied behind me."

"You're wrong, Angelo," I said, cutting in, "all wrong. I agree with you on just one thing: the kid beat you on the up and up. But there's even a catch to that. He let you beat yourself. That's why I say you're a joke only if you quit, only if you sell out Mike and yourself and all the rest of us who believe in you because of one bad drubbing.

"Here," I said, "take a look at these. See what 'The Rag' thinks about you. And then read what Borden has to say. Go ahead, dammit. Look!"

Angelo did. When he finished, I looked him up and down. Then I said, "Remember this, Angelo: champions don't dog it. They don't put their tails between their legs and go ki-yiing off when the going gets rough."

The blood drained from the young prize fighter's face. It was strange. Angelo could berate himself, the *Rag* could do it, and the import of the words wouldn't register. But the strong, plain words of a friend were like a lash. They bit deep.

White-faced, Angelo asked, "Are you calling me a coward, Mr. Evans?"

"No, Angelo," I said, "I'm not calling you a coward. I'm calling you a champ. But I'm also trying to make you understand that it's up to you to prove it. We can't."

Angelo wavered. Five or six agonizing seconds passed before I knew the words had struck home.

"All right," Angelo said suddenly. "I will! By God, I will!" His dark eyes had cleared; the doubt, the self-pitying hurt had left them.

Mike grabbed my hand and almost crushed it. "God bless you, Charley. God bless you."

"Roughhouse," I said sternly, weak-kneed with relief, "go blow your nose!"

It took the Angel another three months to get back to anywhere near normal, to regain his timing and confidence, to get over being glove-shy. Then the word got around and fat Joe Fisch paid the gym a visit and watched the new Angelo in action.

29

"Irish," Fisch said, "your boy's ready!"

Mike beamed.

The two of them lined up three quick fights for Angelo with rated boys and Angelo won them all—by a knockout. He definitely was on his way to the top.

Every chance he got or could contrive, a jubilant Borden was telling the sports world in his own inimitable way: "I told you characters so!" Simultaneously he and the *Rag's* sports staff were waging their own personal Donnybrook over Angelo's prospects. Daily, from ambush, both sides were firing their big guns. At the office we began to call Borden "the General."

The champ had been signed for a title defense against a tough, right-hand puncher named Tiger George Glade, a fast-risen, take-three-to-give-one sensation who had been kayoing all comers. The scrap was to be held in our local stadium under Fisch's high-flying promotional banner. On my advice Mike had ducked a fight for Angelo with Glade a few weeks earlier. Angelo hadn't liked it.

"I can beat Glade," he'd bitterly protested. "If I can't, then I don't rate a title go."

Venomously "The Rag" had said the same thing, putting the spurs to Borden in the process.

Borden had almost had a stroke when he'd learned I was the reason Glade and Angelo hadn't been matched. He'd screamed I was selling him out. "Didja ever stop and think that your paper'll make a monkey's behind outta me if Glade wins?" he'd howled.

"And did it ever occur to you," I'd replied wearily, "that I might have some faint idea what I'm doing?"

"You'd better, Evans. You'd better!"

Charming little egomaniac, this boss of mine. Such a thoughtful, considerate little monster.

What I was betting on, of course, was that Glade would never come close to winning the title.

The Tiger was bait.

One afternoon, a week before the champ and Glade were to collide, I was at the champ's training quarters just outside the city, gathering material for my column. General Borden hadn't stopped breathing down my neck. He wanted gore; I was getting it. The champ was bombing sparring partners insensible with what amounted to almost monotonous regularity when a fat moon-faced member of his entourage came waddling from one of the main buildings, puffing and shouting.

"It's off, Champ! It's off!"

The champ stopped cannonading sparring partner No. 5, a big ponderous heavyweight.

"What's off?" he growled.

"Yer fight with Glade. I just got it over the phone. Some loud-mouthed character they hired to work out with him just sent him to the hospital."

I checked. It was true.

The kid was back in town, and he'd tamed the Tiger. In fact, he'd almost killed him, after taunting Glade into attempting homicide himself. As he was leaving Glade's camp, a reporter and a photographer team from "The Rag" had tried to stop him. The kid had told them to beat it and they'd made the mistake of trying to muscle a story and some pictures. The kid hadn't muscled. He'd roughed the enterprising pair up a bit and smashed their camera. They'd blown the whistle on him and were pressing simple assault and battery charges. The kid was being held in our fancy new escape-proof jail. His bail had been set at $500.

This time, after my talk with Dr. Tom Layton, I was primed and ready. I moved fast, first sending a runner on the double with a hastily scribbled note for the kid. In it, I identified myself and asked the kid to look me up. I said I had a proposition that would interest him, with no strings attached. Then, by phone, I arranged for the kid to make bail. Next I called a booking sergeant friend at the jail. I had a favor to ask—that the kid be released quietly, out a back, basement exit.

These developments and the column I quickly hammered out, hinting at momentous things to come, gladdened Borden's heart. "That's my boy!" he exclaimed. I didn't know whether he meant me or the kid. Right then I didn't much care. I had too many other things on my mind.

"Mine too," I said, and grinned slyly.

"Whaddaya mean by that?" Borden wanted to know.

"You'll see," I told him. "But I'll tell you this much, General: I'm tired of just reporting and interpreting sports news. I think for a change I'll make some."

I left Borden scratching his bald head and muttering to himself. My first stop was a phone booth. I called my booking sergeant friend at the jail. The kid had been given my note and released without any fanfare. Good. Good so far.

31

The kid might run but I didn't think he would. That was part of the gamble. If I'd gone to him, I'd have got nowhere.

I dropped another dime into the slot and dialed Dr. Tom Layton's number. I brought him up to date.

"Tom," I said, "wish me luck. I think I'm going to need plenty of it."

Chapter Seven

WIND WHIPPED ALONG the concrete canyon called Main Street. Big drops of rain spattered against the glass-windowed front of the building. Traffic was light. Car tires made a whooshing sound as they passed. The multicolored neon lights glowed like fuzzy rainbows.

It was close to 11 P.M. and I'd almost given up. I'd been sitting at the bar in Clancy's for four hours, nursing along a succession of beers.

And waiting. Anxiously.

I'll give him another thirty minutes, I thought, flicking up my left coat sleeve and taking another look at my wrist watch.

Twenty of those minutes ticked away. Then someone tapped me on the shoulder. I turned.

"You looking for me, mister?"

It was the kid, but a changed kid. Only that half-sardonic, half-laughing smile and the cheap jacket, T-shirt, and jeans were the same. He was thinner. A jagged, purplish scar extended from the corner of his mouth to his right ear. His nose had been smashed since I'd last seen him and now one eyelid drooped slightly. There was fresh scar tissue over the cold, gray-green eyes.

Take him as you find him, on his own terms, Tom Layton had cautioned me. *Don't under any circumstances try to sell him a bill of goods. And be prepared for a shock.*

I hid the shock.

"You're a hard guy to find," I said. "I've been looking for you for a long time. Where you been keeping yourself?"

"Around."

"Hungry?"

"Yeah."

"Good. Then let's get out of here and go get something to eat. I'm starved."

There was a small, all-night eatery up the street where

33

I ate most of my meals and where we wouldn't be disturbed.

"My coupé's parked at the curb," I said.

"Let's go," the kid said.

We made a dash for my car through the rain. The kid didn't say anything on the way to the restaurant or during the meal of steak, french fries, salad, and pie, which he wolfed. Then he took my note out of his pocket and smoothed it out.

"You're a newspaper guy, aren't you, mister?"

"A sports columnist," I acknowledged.

"I don't like newspaper guys," the kid said. "Most of 'em are phonies. That's why I almost didn't show up. I couldn't figure out what you wanted with me or how come you got me sprung. That made me curious." The kid's voice lost its conversational tone with calculated abruptness. "What's your angle, mister?"

I shook my head. "No angle."

Our eyes locked.

The kid grinned with deceptive mildness. "I wouldn't like it worth a damn if you tried to shoot any fast ones at me, mister. Just lay it on the line. What's on your mind?"

"You," I said simply.

The tenseness, the sudden, wary hostility was like a wall, and the kid retreated behind it.

He said very softly, "What about me?"

"I could say everything about you."

"And I could tell you to go to hell. I ain't interested in getting my name in the papers."

"I know that."

"Then what's this all about?"

"When I asked you to look me up I was hoping you'd tell me about yourself and what made you mad at the world."

"It wouldn't interest you."

"I think it would."

Defiance blazed in the kid's eyes like gray-green fire.

"Okay, then I'll put it another way and maybe you'll understand. It's none of your damned business! You newspaper bastards are all alike. You all got nose trouble. All you know how to do is pry. Well, mister, I got news for you. You picked the wrong guy this time. So don't push your luck."

"Son, you don't seem to understand. I'm not trying to pry. I want to help you."

34

"Who the hell says I need help?"

"I do."

Scowling, the kid thought this over. "Mister, do you know what I feel like doing?"

I nodded. "Yes, son, I do. But I'm a comparatively old man by your standards and you don't fight old men, do you? You whack me around and it doesn't prove anything. Besides, be honest with yourself, you're up against a problem you can't lick with your fists. You didn't solve it when you clobbered Angelo and then Glade and that delightful pair from "The Rag" and God knows how many other people. And now it's got you surrounded, hasn't it?"

"You're doing the talking, mister."

That was right. I was doing the talking. And I had to keep on. Because all I had was words. They might or might not be enough.

I continued: "You can feel it closing in on you, getting closer and closer. It's like something out of a nightmare, isn't it? The more you fight it and hate it, the worse it gets, the more it tries to strangle you. And do you know why, son? Because it's inside you and because you've been afraid to jerk it out and see it for exactly what it is."

The kid didn't reply immediately. He sat there and stared at me unblinkingly. At length he said. "You seem to know a lot, mister."

But not enough—yet. I had to get the kid talking.

"Why don't you tell me the rest of it?" I urged. "No harm in that. Then maybe together we'll be able to work something out. At least it ought to be worth a try. I give you my word. You can trust me."

"I probably can. But I don't want to. I don't ever want to trust anybody again."

"It's no good going on as you have been."

"Goddamn you," the kid said.

"You've got guts," I said. "You've got guts enough to look inside yourself."

"Goddamn you," the kid said again.

He began to sweat, his forehead glistened with perspiration, as the nightmare he'd kept buried slowly ate its way to the surface of his mind. One part of him tried to fight it back, to will it back, to curse it back—and couldn't. Like a strong, fuming acid, its searing action couldn't be halted until it was wholly free of its dark inner prison.

The kid's face twisted grotesquely, resembling the face of

35

a man I once had witnessed undergoing insulin shock. The image flickered, beginning to come into focus. The kid half-stood, rising in a kind of atavistic crouch. He looked wildly around. I thought for an instant he might go berserk. Then the image was in full focus and the kid saw it; he saw it for what it was.

Slowly he sat down.

"All right," he said hoarsely. "Okay, mister. I'll tell you. But don't laugh. Don't laugh, mister. God help you if you laugh."

"I won't laugh."

The kid was silent a moment, hunched over the table, searching for the right words.

"Ever since I was a little guy," he finally began, "I've been having a fight with myself. And you know something, mister? It's been a lot worse than any fight I ever had with anybody else. Like I said, you seem to know a lot, a helluva lot. But can you understand that? Tell me, can you *really* understand it."

"I can understand it," I said.

I could—now that I'd talked with Dr. Tom Layton. The mind doctors called it ambivalence; the witch doctors, demon possession.

In the next hour and a half the kid told me the story of his life and later I was able to check most of it out. It wasn't a pretty story. It could have been a chapter from one of Dr. Tom Layton's textbooks; only, told in the kid's own words rather than in the special, occasionally incomprehensible language of the clinician, and related with a savage candor, it was more grippingly personal, more tragically terrible than anything found in any text.

For those ninety minutes, I became the kid, I saw the world through his eyes; I knew its mocking, senseless barbarism, its warlike visage, its violence, its profanation of hope and love and faith.

Most importantly of all, I learned the meaning of hate; I discovered what it meant to be fury-driven.

36

Chapter Eight

As IT ALMOST INVARIABLY DOES, the gross personality warping had begun in childhood.

Then the kid was wild-bird shy and stick thin. He lived in a rundown tenement section of a big industrial city. There wasn't always enough to eat. The kid's old man was an over-sized, mean ex-pug who had hit the skids and the bottle. He missed the adulation and the roar of the crowd, the spot-light. A coarse and cruel guy who resented suddenly finding himself a forgotten nobody, he drank, brawled, and phi-landered. He had a habit, too, of coming home and beating his wife, the kid, and the kid's younger sister, Janey. While he beat him, the old man would roar at the kid that he had to learn to take it. The kid would be terrified. When his father left, his mother would hold him in her arms and re-assure him. He worshiped his small, still pretty, work-worn mother.

She asked the children to be patient with their father. He had been different once, she told them. Smiling. Happy. Kind, even, in his rough way. And generous. She remembered him as she had seen him through the eyes of young love, when he had been on top. She wanted desperately to believe he one day would be like that again. And she often asked herself whether it was possibly some failure on her part which had made her life and that of the children a nightmare. Why, why had he changed so? The truth eluded her.

His cruelty became more pronounced. The quarrels they had were more frequent and violent. It seemed she could do nothing to please him. Once he shouted at her, "What the hell'd you marry me for in the first place?"

"Because you asked me to and because I loved you," she answered. That was the fact.

"Love!" he exclaimed obliquely. "You don't know the meaning of the word." He leered. "You think layin' on your back and spreadin' your legs is love?"

37

Her face turned scarlet. "Fred! Please! Don't talk like that in front of the children."

He roared with laughter, then his coarse face grew hard and cruel. "Christ," he said blasphemously, "you always did think sex was something dirty."

"Oh, God," she said.

"That's it," he said, "start prayin'. Tell the Old Guy with a Beard what a rotten bastard your husband is. Feel sorry for yourself. Go ahead. And while you're at it I think I'll go down to the corner beer joint and have a beer."

He took the kid with him. He knew that would make her sick with worry. On the way the kid forced himself to tell his old man, no matter how timidly, that he thought it was wrong to treat his mother the way he did.

"You've got no right to do it," he blurted out, cringing as he uttered the words.

The old man jerked to a halt. "Well, I'll be damned!" he said aloud, staring down at the kid. "So you think you're big enough to start telling me what to do, do you?"

"I only . . ." Fear tied the kid's tongue.

"You only what?"

"I just don't think it's right," he blurted.

"Now isn't that touching," the old man said sarcastically. "You just don't think it's right. What kind of a goddamned little fool have I got for a son?" he demanded rhetorically. "Well, now's a good time to find out." The look on his face wasn't paternal. "Come on," he told the kid. . . .

"Beer for me and a straight whisky for the kid," the old man told the bartender.

"Jeez, Fred, you know I could lose my license if I got caught serving a minor. How about giving him a root beer?"

"I said a straight whisky for the kid and quit cryin' about what could happen," the old man said. His mood had turned ugly. The bartender realized he might tear the place up if crossed.

"Sure, Fred, sure."

The kid looked at the shot glass on the bar in front of him.

"Drink it," he was told.

"I don't want to."

"Drink it or I'll kick you all the way home."

The kid drank it—and gagged. His throat burned.

His old man shook a cigarette out of his pack. "Here."

"Please, Dad," the kid said. "You know I don't smoke."

"Here!"

The kid took the cigarette and put it slowly to his lips. He puffed mechanically when his old man put a match to its tip. His old man told him to inhale. He did. The smoke made him sick, deathly sick.

"Now let's go," his old man said.

"I think I'm going to throw up."

His old man shoved him roughly into the men's room. "Go ahead. Heave your damn guts out."

The kid retched until he was almost too weak to stand. He was afraid. His face mirrored his fear. It brought a cruel mocking smile to his father's lips.

"Maybe this'll teach you part of the score. But I doubt it. I doubt if you got the guts."

"I'm never going to drink or smoke!" the kid cried defiantly. (He never did.)

"Why not?"

"Because."

"Because you're a damned little pansy."

"I'm not."

"We'll see."

Butch, a neighbor's son, was a year younger than the kid. He was a tough kid, a gutter-bred youngster, who thought the kid's swaggering, hard-drinking old man was a type worth emulating. He lived with his widowed mother, spending most of his time running with a gang. Butch had often come close to whipping the kid but had refrained only because of his perverted hero worship of the kid's old man.

They walked to Butch's.

"See if he's home," the father ordered. "If he is, tell him to come down here. I want to talk to him."

Butch swaggered down the walk, a cigarette butt dangling from the corner of his mouth.

"Hi, Fred," he said. "You wanta see me?"

"Yeah, I do. My kid here's been telling me you're a lot of hot air. He says he can kick your ass any day in the week. You think he's right?"

The kid trembled at this betrayal.

"Hell no, I don't think he's right. Christ, you yourself taught me most of what I know about using my dukes and never givin' the chump a chance." Butch glared at the kid. He spit out the butt.

"I didn't say it," the kid managed to get out.

"You callin' me a liar?" the old man asked ominously.

"No," the kid stammered.

"Then you said it."

"I didn't!"

"That ain't no way to talk to your old man," Butch said, swaggering toward the kid.

Involuntarily the kid took a couple of steps back. There was a dryness in his mouth, a tightening in his belly. He gulped, trying to swallow the fear.

"I don't want to fight you, Butch," he blurted out.

"What're you shakin' for?" Butch asked. He grinned cruelly. "You let your mouth overload your ass, and now you're shakin' like a dog tryin' to shit peach seeds."

"There's no reason for us to fight," the kid said desperately, hating himself because fear was making him beg.

"Goddammit," the old man roared, "quit whining. Do your talking with your dukes. If you're any part of a man, a little tail-kicking ain't gonna kill you."

Butch stood in front of the kid, grinning, and he seemed to grow and grow until he filled most of the universe. "You heard what your old man said, didn't you?"

Butch blurred. The ground beneath him began to heave. "I feel sick," the kid said. "I want to go home."

Then, at a signal from his old man, Butch hit him. The blow crunched against his jaw and upended him. He fell in a heap to the ground. He heard the sobs but it took him a few seconds to realize they were coming from his own throat.

"Get up!" his father shouted. "Get up and fight or I'll kick your goddamned head off."

The kid scrambled to his feet. Instead of fighting, he tried to run. His old man tripped him and he sprawled headlong. He cowered down. His breath was as hot as fire. It burned his lungs. Hysteria seized him with clawlike hands.

The next thing he knew his father had jerked him to his feet and, while holding him with one big hand, was slapping him with the other, regularly, almost rhythmically.

"Shut up! I said shut up!"

Off in the distance, in an echo chamber, a reedy voice kept screaming:

"No! No! No!"

When the kid clamped his mouth shut, the voice was stifled, and then, gradually receding, only the echo in his mind was audible. It died out slowly.

40

Butch was round-eyed. "Jeez, Fred, what happened? Did he have a fit?"

"I dunno. It looks to me like the gutless little bastard blew his top when you belted him."

"I want to go home," the kid said. He began to retch again.

"Don't worry," the old man said, "that's where we're going. I don't want people to see you around me."

At home the kid's mother threw her arms around her son. She asked accusingly, "Fred, what have you done to Buddy?"

"I ain't done anything," the kid's old man said sullenly. "It's what you've done. You made a damn pansy outta him. He ain't got a gut in his body. Sometimes I wonder if he's really mine. You sure one of those Gospel-spouting characters you're always sneaking off to see didn't fill you full of more'n just holy talk?"

The old man leered. In his cheap and crude league that was clever talk. Just wait'll he told his beer joint cronies!

Obscenely the question hung in the air.

Color flamed in his wife's face. She released her son, gently pushed him from her, then faced her husband.

"You animal," she said.

The kid shared his mother's sudden shame. Before, he had only feared his father. He still feared him; but now he hated him, too. He would never forgive his old man that question. And the hate would grow and take shape, spawned by that interrogative obscenity, and in time, a voracious thing, it would consume the fear. Then it would seek to devour love—and sanity.

"Sure I'm an animal," the old man said, laughing coarsely. "And the difference between me and you is that I got sense enough and guts enough to admit it. You haven't. You keep trying to kid yourself that you're something special, that the Old Guy with the Beard is upstairs watching what's going on and that someday you're going to be up there playing a harp for him and walking those golden streets."

"You're drunk."

"Drunk? Not this time. But what if I was? I get tanked up on alcohol and you stay loaded on religion. That makes us even, the way I figure it."

"Sometimes I think you actually want me to hate you."

"Maybe I do. And you know why? Because then you got a little life and fire in you. Then you're more'n just a sexless thing with a damn martyr complex."

41

"At least I'd think you would try to act like a man in front of the children."

"You want me to act like a man in front of the children, huh? Fine. Thanks for the invitation. I'll do just that. Now come here!"

"What do you want?"

"What the hell do you think I want? You, that's what."

"Do you mean . . .?"

"Yeah, what else? And stop acting so goddamned shocked. It's what you want too, only you're too damn hoity-toity to admit it."

"Fred!"

"Oh, Fred, my aching ass! Come here!"

The kid's mother swayed on her feet. Briefly she closed her eyes. When she opened them, she looked at her towering mate with unconcealed loathing. "I didn't believe you could be so bestial," she said tonelessly.

"Hell," the kid's old man said, "a man's entitled to a piece at home now and then, ain't he?" His obscene laughter could have come from the bowels of Hades.

The mother prayed, her lips moving soundlessly.

The old man turned to the kid. "Well, what do you think you're going to do, stand around and watch? You want to see how it's done, I suppose. I remember when you took that look before."

"No!" the kid blurted out, denying, protesting.

"Come to think about it," his old man said, "I guess you ain't any longer interested in learning how a man does it, at that. The pansy's got another way."

"Dad!" the kid cried in shame and agony, squirming as though he had been skewered. "Don't talk like that!"

"Why not?" the old man roared, taking malicious pleasure in baiting them both unmercifully. When he started, it was almost impossible for him to stop. Something satanic drove him to hurt them as much as he could. Jealousy was part of it, an unreasoning fear and suspicion that they secretly hated him; that they had drawn a circle and left him out. So he hurt them, he said, to make them sorry. Yet he told himself he didn't care how they felt. He sneered at what he called their softness. Being able to take it, and taking what you wanted when you wanted it, was what mattered. Being tough, too, and being boss. Being *male*. Sex was not only a form of crude pleasure; it was also a means of in-

42

flicting retribution and an orgiastic affirmation that profane "love" was the only kind there really was. It actually was not love at all but simply lust, and one of its ingredients was hate, self-hate. So they thought he was hard and vicious. Well, by God, he'd show them! He'd show them how right they were and in the process he'd prove how weak and stupid they were, how easily dominated.

Why not?

"Because," the kid said. "Because—it isn't right."

"Well, stop me then. I say that might's right, goddammit, and I'm going to keep on saying it and anything else I please until somebody shows me I'm wrong. And on top of that, I'm going to do what I goddamn well please until somebody that's big enough comes along and stops me. You ain't big enough. You're only big enough to take orders and now I'm ordering you to quit mewling. If you don't I'll give you the beating of your life."

"You'd better leave, Buddy," the kid's mother told him, aware that her husband had worked himself up to the point of violence.

"All right, Mother," the kid said. "If you want me to." He turned to go.

The kick lifted the kid at least a foot off the floor. He staggered and fell with a cry, his pain almost more than he could stand. Dimly he heard his mother's stifled scream and then the angry boom of his old man's voice. "It ain't what she says," he shouted. "It's what I say. I'm the boss around here. Remember that. Now get out and be goddamn quick about it."

The kid scrambled to his feet and scurried out. When the door slammed behind him he stopped. Fearfully he tiptoed back to the door and listened. The sound of his mother's quiet sobs and choked, monosyllabic replies faintly reached his ears. Clearly he heard then the arrogant, thundered command of his old man to her: "Get your clothes off!" It occurred to him, and the realization was like a whiplash, that probably his old man had intended him to hear. For what more cunningly effective way was there to drive the most telling wedge of all between them, mother and son? What more insidious dialectic could be contrived than this one, with its subtle, terrible imagery?

The kid's physical pain was blotted out in that instant. It was replaced by an exquisite mental agony—and a revela-

43

tion. He shuddered. His tears stopped, but perspiration drenched his thin body, his broad forehead.

Before, the kid had not understood his old man. Now he did, not perfectly and completely but with a terrifying flash of insight that threw their tense relationship into shadowed, black and white relief. Biologically they might be father and son, but psychologically they weren't. Psychologically they were deadly competitors, and what they competed for was the woman in their lives, the wife and the mother.

You can't have her! his old man was saying behaviorally. *I won't share her with you because if I do you'll try to shut me out altogether. Already you've tried to do that. But you aren't going to get away with it even if I have to make you both hate me. I am the male in this family; I am the one who is all-powerful, and it was my maleness and my power that gave you existence in the first place. You've overlooked that but I haven't. Now, because you would dethrone me, because you would rob me of what is rightfully mine, I will use these weapons against you, against all of us. If necessary, in my own way, slowly and ruthlessly, I'll destroy us; and I'll take animal [sexual] pleasure in my act. And you'll be helpless to stop me unless you get like I am and share my private hell of [self-]hate and doubt and damnation.*

There had been other times in the past when these major battles—in a personality "war" that, once declared, could never be concluded on honorable terms—had ended with the kid's old man forcing his wife to submit to him, sneering openly all the while at her simultaneous shame and involuntary physical response, enjoying perversely, too, the degradation the act imposed on them both. On each occasion the tension had driven him to humiliate her and the kid more, to outrage their physical selves and their sensibilities until they, in turn, would be driven to rebel. So far he had been unable to precipitate a final crisis. He had succeeded only in securing a brief respite from the tension.

Once the kid had entered his parents' bedroom when his old man had his mother on the bed. A bitter, deep need to confirm the truth, disguised as childish curiosity, had been the magnet which had drawn him. Before averting his eyes, stammering an unintelligible apology, and running out, he saw their nude bodies locked together, his old man on top, breathing heavily and jerkily. Their movements were primitive. Her eyes glazed, his mother moaned softly; then, seeing him, she gasped and brought a hand to her guilt-contorted face. "What the hell!" his old man snorted, jerking his head around in time to see his son running out. The old man's Rabelaisian laughter followed him first into the front room and then out into the street. He couldn't run fast enough to get away from it, nor, no matter how hard he tried, could he erase from his mind the scene he had witnessed.

That was sex, and sex was bad; it was dirty. Profane. Worse, more frightening, sex might be loved unmasked. It raised the possibility that what his mother had taught him was wrong, an illusion to conceal a jungle truth. For wasn't she, and wasn't he, forced always to do what the old man ordered? How could there be verity in the Christian truths she had taught him when those who tried to live by them were ever at the mercy of the hate-driven, the hell-haunted, the worshipers of violence, and the captive warriors of degeneracy?

You gotta be able to take it! That was the sermon his old man always preached. And the words assumed a new and insidious significance when, following the bedroom incident and the doubt and fears it spawned, he first was alone with his mother. The acute embarrassment each felt forestalled an immediate resumption of their intimacy. Sadly the kid was forced to recognize that his mother was not a perfect vessel. She had been dirtied, damaged, robbed of her purity. Her goodness, her faith hadn't been enough to protect her. Recognizing this was the beginning of his education in learning to take it, in accepting the fact that life could be ugly, sordid, brutal, and that the meek often were left unblessed unless you could say that a kick and a sneer were blessings.

Now the kid stood at the door of their tenement home and added to the fund of his knowledge: for all his old man's apparent toughness, his crude dominance, his violent power, his seeming contempt of God, man, and the devil, his old man feared him, the skinny, frightened son who couldn't defend himself physically, who tearfully had vowed he would never smoke or drink, who was a mama's boy, a sissy. He, the father, feared him, the son, so much he was doing his blasphemous damnedest to make the kid a carbon copy of him—and succeeding, in a hellishly subtle way.

For the doubt had been planted, and the hate. The old man had committed finally an act the kid could not, would

45

not, forgive or forget. The kid would tell his mother this—
and the old man's fate would be sealed.

It would be then only a matter of time. And the irony was
that, without knowing it, they would be racing the clock.

Chapter Nine

THE KID AND HIS SISTER Janey found a tiny kitten someone had abandoned. "Of course you can keep it," their mother said. They were thrilled. It was the first pet they had ever had. But when their father returned home, ugly-drunk, he threw the kitten out. "There's enough mouths to feed around here now," he growled. Yet that wasn't the reason and they knew it. They knew he was being arbitrary and mean, purposely cruel.

Janey cried and retrieved the kitten, clutching it desperately. She begged to be allowed to keep it. "I'll share my food with him, Father. He won't be any trouble at all," she pleaded.

The old man snatched the kitten away from her and shouted, "You'll learn to mind, by God!" Then he did a sickening thing. He filled a bucket with water and drowned the kitten in it, making them watch. When the little thing ceased its pitiful struggling and the air bubbles no longer rose to the surface, their old man threw the small wet body at their feet. "There's your goddamned pet," he sneered. "Go ahead and play with it now. Pet it and listen to it purr." He laughed.

Janey's eyes had dilated with horror. "I hate you!" she screamed. "I hate you! I hate you!"

She was beaten.

The kid's old man repeatedly struck Janey and shouted, "Shut up! Shut up!"

"I won't!" Janey cried. "I hate you! I hate you!"

The old man became so enraged he doubled up his fist and slammed it into Janey's chest. Luckily the old man was drunk, and off balance. Therefore, the blow broke no bones and did no permanent damage, although it sent her crashing across the room and dumped her in a sobbing heap in a corner. At that point their mother sought to intervene. She, too, was knocked to the floor. The kid stood petrified with fear.

47

He burned with shame because he didn't have the courage to stand up to his father.

The kid's old man glared at his son. "I suppose you don't like it either?" he challenged. "Well!"

"I . . . I . . ." the kid stammered. *I hate you! I hate you too!* he wanted to spit out at his parent. But the words wouldn't come. They lodged in his throat. He could only stand there and tremble.

The old man snorted. "Hell, I keep forgetting I got a goddamned sniveling coward for a son," he said in drunken disgust. Then he clomped heavily into the bathroom and was sick. He began to vomit—and curse the world, fleeting fame, cheap whisky, marriage, offspring, stray kittens, even himself. It was as though, with the alcoholic contents of his stomach, he was endeavoring to regurgitate the revulsion he felt for his muddled and monstrous existence. Audibly, in this unguarded moment, he cried out: "What the hell has happened to me?"

It was a question only his death would be able to answer; he would never know.

Janey rose, crossed the room, and gently picked up the dead kitten. Huge tears rolled down her cheeks as she told the small wet body she was sorry.

The kid crept to his dazed mother. He stroked her hair with his hand. "Mama!" he said. "Oh, Mama!"

His mother tried to smile.

After breakfast the next morning the kid's mother asked him and Janey to go to the living room. "I'd like to speak to your father alone," she said.

In the living room Janey whispered, "Do you think there'll be another fight?"

"I don't know," the kid said.

"He looked awful mean and he kept looking at all of us real funny," Janey commented.

The kid nodded. "Let's listen."

"All right. But we'll have to be careful and not let him catch us."

Standing close to the kitchen door, they overheard their mother say, "Don't ever beat the children again, Fred."

"You trying to tell me how to raise my own kids?" For him, his tone was surprisingly mild. These mornings after, he would feel a guilt of sorts that found expression in sullenness. But press him and he would take refuge in anger. It was his belief, or so he claimed, that only weaklings ever admitted they had been wrong.

"They're mine, too," their mother replied reasonably.

"Somebody's gotta teach them the facts of life," their old man said, going on the defensive, a warning tinge of anger in his voice. He added, "You won't. All you ever do is fill their heads with a lot of turn-the-other-cheek Bible talk."

"That's better than trying to turn them into vicious little savages, which you'd do if you had your way."

"They gotta learn to take it. They gotta learn like I did, the hard way." He was trying to match her reasonableness.

"Being coarse and cruel to one's children doesn't strike me as the best way to teach them anything."

"What's got into you, anyway?" he demanded sharply, suspiciously.

"Drowning that kitten was the final straw. You shouldn't have done it."

"Goddammit, Helen, are you trying to threaten me?" Rarely did he ever call her by her given name. Usually it was just a peremptory "you."

"Threatening *you*, Fred?"

"I don't like the way you're talking," he said. "I don't like any part of it."

"Just don't ever beat the children again, Fred."

"I'm the one that gives the orders around this place and don't you forget it."

"Don't beat them, Fred."

"Oh, for Christ's sake, shut up! You sound like a broken record."

"I want you to understand, Fred. I don't want you to make any mistake."

"Yeah, and what happens if I do give 'em a whipping?"

"Don't do it, Fred. I'm giving you fair warning."

Their old man let out a bellow and came to his feet so suddenly he upset the breakfast table. Its contents crashed to the floor. Blind with rage, he roared, "Get it through your thick head that I'll damn well beat those brats of ours any time I figure they need a beating, whether you like it or not!" He pounded into the living room as the kid and Janey flattened themselves against the wall near the door, paused only long enough to grab his coat, and then stomped out, cursing all the time. The sound of him in the hallway died out.

It grew quiet.

"I guess he's gone," the kid said, speaking in a whisper for fear his old man might hear him and return.

Their mother had him and Janey dress in their best clothes and then she took them to church. It wasn't Sunday, the only day their old man grudgingly allowed them to go, but she took them anyway. The small, plain church was deserted.

"I want you to pray for me, children," she said in a voice that had a faraway sound to it. "Ask God to give me the strength to do what I must."

On his knees, facing the altar, the kid closed his eyes and prayed with silent, earnest desperation. *Please, God, don't make my mother suffer any more. Help her. You just have to. That isn't asking too much, is it, God? You know how hard she's had it and how good she is. And now if You don't give her a hand I'm afraid something terrible's going to happen.*

After they had returned home and had changed into their old play clothes, their mother sent them off on an errand. In their absence she borrowed an old pistol from a neighbor. The kid wasn't supposed to know but he found out and was filled with dread.

"Mother's got a gun!" he whispered in awe to Janey.

"What?"

"I saw it when I went into her bedroom to look for a shirt she said she was going to iron for me. I thought it might've got put in with his shirts. Then I saw this gun when I looked in the dresser."

"What gun?"

"It's old Mr. Rayne's, I'm positive. He's let me look at it a couple of times."

"Then what's Mom doing with it?"

"I don't know, unless . . ."

Janey's eyes grew saucer-wide. She said breathlessly, "Do you think she'd use it on him?"

"I don't know. Remember, she told him never to beat us again and you know he said he's going to."

"I remember. What do you think we should do?"

"I'm not sure. I got my head dizzy trying to figure something out."

Janey suggested, "You could sneak the gun out and hide it."

"But we're really not sure why it's even there," the kid pointed out. "So it might be a mistake to take it. Maybe

50

there's a good reason it's there that doesn't have anything to do with Mom's argument with him."

"If there is," Janey said scornfully, "I'd like to know what it is."

"I didn't say there was," the kid defended; "I just said maybe there was."

"Well, we ought to do something," Janey said.

"You leave it to me," the kid told her. "And promise me you won't say anything to anybody about it."

"All right, Buddy, I promise."

Janey kept her word. She didn't say anything. But neither did the kid do anything. In the middle of that night he was still awake, thinking. He remembered with a chilling clarity the last sentence of his prayer: *And now if You don't give her a hand I'm afraid something terrible's going to happen.* Lying there in the darkness, full of fear and wonder, the kid was certain God had elected to intervene. He had made the kid His instrument by divulging to him the fact and whereabouts of the gun.

It's like Janey said, he thought. *All I have to do is grab the gun when Mom isn't around and ditch it somewhere.*

And he'd do it! he vowed with vehemence out of all proportion to the simple act to be done. He'd do it the first thing in the morning. He wouldn't wait an extra minute. As soon as his mother was in the kitchen getting breakfast he would sneak into the bedroom and get the gun. That was settled, final.

He got down on his knees beside his cot for the second time that night. "Thank you, God, for answering my prayer and letting me know what to do," he said, his voice thick with emotion.

But when he got back in bed and tried to go to sleep the Devil tapped him on the shoulder. "Haven't you forgotten something, my noble young man?" the Devil said.

"What's that?" the kid wanted to know, trembling.

"Your mother's request. Her exact words were: 'Ask God to give me the strength to do what I must.' How do you know that ventilating your old man with that revolver wasn't what she was asking strength for?"

The kid had a ready answer: "Because my mother's a good woman and she believes in the Ten Commandments."

"Granted," replied the Devil. "But what has it got her? You know as well as I do. Nothing but pain, poverty, misery, and humiliation. So now you're telling me you want her to

51

keep on getting more of the same. That must be it or you'd leave that gun where it is." The Devil added contemptuously, "You're a fine son!"

"But she'll get in trouble," the kid said.

"Ridiculous," the Devil snorted. "Don't you give her credit for having any sense at all? Stop and think. Use your head. She's told your old man not to beat you or your sister any more. Well, she knows and you know that he's the kind of bullheaded fool who'd give you a beating now just to prove nobody gives him orders. And when he starts, *Kapow!* he's a goner. And she's got the perfect alibi. No jury in the world would ever convict a godly woman like your mother of killing some no-good and oversized brute like your old man, not after a smart attorney gets up and tells them what kind of a guy he was. They're more apt to give her a medal."

"But . . ."

"But you're scared, scared to death," the Devil said scathingly. "That's it, isn't it? You're afraid of what might happen *to you*. You think somehow you might get hurt. Actually you hate your old man's guts but *you* haven't got the guts to admit it even to yourself. If you really cared about your mother and sister you'd leave that gun there. You'd let your mother send your old man to me as soon as she got a chance. The place for him is in Hell and he's long overdue. But *you* want to keep him around. And then you've got the nerve, the gall, to pass off a yard-wide yellow streak as piety. Well, you're not fooling me and there'll be snow on my doorstep before this night's over if I don't find a way of letting the world know that you're nothing but a phony little coward without an ounce of manhood in you!"

"I'm not a coward! I'm not!"

"Then prove it!"

"I will! I will! I'll show you!"

His mother shook him again and he opened his eyes. "Wake up, Buddy," she said urgently. "Wake up."

"I'm awake."

"Are you all right?"

"Yes," he said. "It was just a bad dream."

"A nightmare," his mother corrected. "You woke Janey and me up when you began to shout."

"I'm sorry."

The kid's old man didn't come home for another three days. When he did he was broke, hungover, and in an ugly,

52

black mood, spoiling for trouble. He claimed he'd left some money in a bureau drawer and it was gone. He accused first his wife and then the kid and Janey of taking it. Actually there had been no money left there; it had been spent days before, with his knowledge, but he wouldn't listen.

"I'll find out who took that money if I have to beat the truth out of all of you!" he shouted. Then he grabbed the kid, who had been standing, frozen, closest to him. His fingers bit cruelly into the kid's thin shoulder.

"All right, speak up! Did you steal that money?"

"No, sir," the kid said.

"You're lying!"

The kid's head rang from the beefy-handed slap. His mother didn't say a word. Yet her lips moved, as though in prayer, and a fixed look came to her eyes. She turned and walked unhurriedly into the bedroom, returning in a moment with the gun.

"Fred," she said quietly, in a voice that wasn't hers at all, "I told you never to beat the children again. I meant it."

The kid's old man saw the gun. It was held resolutely, if awkwardly, and it was pointed at him. Fear flickered in his bleary eyes, then cunning. An unseen hand pulled the skin tight across his face, giving it the appearance of a jackal's mask. The color drained from it except in two splotchy places on the forehead. He hesitated momentarily, staring at the large round barrel of the gun and knowing that here was the rebellion he had demanded for so long. Now he had to stamp it out, crush it ruthlessly, with guile and violence—or die.

He snatched the kid and held him up in front of him, using him as a shield. His words were wheedling, soft, conciliatory, as he inched toward the gun: "Now, Helen. Now, Helen. Don't do anything you'll be sorry for later. We can talk this over, can't we? Maybe I was wrong about the money."

The kid's mother retreated slowly to the far wall. The old man came closer, closer, until less than four feet separated them. In a blur of movement he hurled the kid aside. Then, almost in the same instant, in the manner of a carnivore that seeks to paralyze its prey with fear, he hurled himself forward with a roar.

The gun also roared—and an invisible fist smashed into the old man's chest, halting his forward motion. He swayed ludicrously, his knees beginning to buckle. "Helen," he gasped, "you shouldn't've done it. Shouldn't've murdered me." He coughed and crashed to the floor, dead, his mouth forming blood and saliva bubbles.

The gun had fallen from the mother's hand. It lay near *his* body, the barrel pointing accusingly at her like a steel finger. All the strength drained from her and she sat down, staring in numb horror at the gun. "Dear God," she whispered, "forgive me."

The acrid odor of cordite filled the room, bit at the kid's nostrils. He got uncertainly and shakily to his feet. While his old man had used him as a shield, a pure terror had stopped his breathing, had almost stopped his heart. When he had been thrown violently aside, the gun had thundered in his ear and for brief moments the world had turned black. Then he had heard his old man's voice; he had opened his eyes as his old man fell.

He's dead! he exulted. *He's dead and I'm glad. He got what was coming to him. He was no good. He was mean and cruel. I hated him.*

Then, both fascinated and repelled by the dead body, the kid thought: *And I showed the Devil I'm not a coward. I proved it by leaving the gun.* But the thought was a mockery, a lie, and he knew it. He knew it when his mother whispered, "Dear God, forgive me." You never proved anything to the Devil; and you certainly never established how brave you were by letting him trick or goad you into doing what he wanted done. Brave men, no matter how young they were, didn't hide behind their mothers. But cowards did. Young fools willing to deceive themselves did. *And I'm both,* the kid thought bitterly. It was too late to be sorry. Being sorry wouldn't bring a dead man back to life.

The police came; first two uniformed officers, then a team of detectives from homicide, and finally the coroner and a matron from the city jail. The cops took pictures of the gun and the corpse, and asked questions. Who did it? Why did you do it? How did it happen? The kid tried to tell them it was his fault but they wouldn't listen then. They didn't want a story, Sonny, they said; they just wanted the facts.

"So you did it, huh?" a big detective named Mulligan said to his mother.

Obviously in a state of shock, she nodded dumbly. "I had to do it," she said, her voice hollow and remote. The statement was intended as neither an apology nor a defense of

54

her homicidal act. Rather, it was offered as an explanation, a fact—but a fact the law in its cold majesty didn't recognize and one the detectives with their authoritarian mentalities were both unable and unwilling to grasp.

She was placed under arrest, then marched to a waiting police car as the press hurled a barrage of questions, and flash bulbs blinded her. The ride to the city prison was a siren-screaming one; she sat stiffly upright in the middle of the back seat, flanked by Mulligan on one side and by the matron on the other, staring sightlessly straight ahead. Only once on the way did she repeat quietly, "I had to do it."

She was booked, fingerprinted, and placed in a cell in the women's quarters with an alcoholic crone charged with forgery.

"And what're you in for, dearie?" the crone asked.

"Murder," answered the tall female turnkey for the kid's mother. "And she doesn't like old ladies who ask questions."

"Murder!" said the crone. "Glory be! What've they done to me?"

As the turnkey walked away, the kid's mother said to herself, looking around, the events catching up with her, "My children. My babies. What will happen to them?"

"Now, now, dearie," the crone said. "Don't you worry about them. They'll be taken good care of. So you just relax."

The kid and Janey were taken to the juvenile hall. The next afternoon Mulligan, accompanied by another detective and a police stenographer, questioned the kid.

"I just got through talking to your mother. She's okay and wanted me to be sure and tell you and Janey hello for her."

"Have you got her in jail?" the kid asked.

"Hell, son," Mulligan said uneasily. "We got a job to do."

"You ought to let her go. It's really not her fault that it happened, it's mine. I tried to tell you last night but you wouldn't listen." The kid added desperately, "Now you *have* to listen."

Mulligan smiled reassuringly. "That's what I'm here for—to listen. Now you just go ahead and tell me the whole story."

"I knew she'd borrowed the gun. I had a chance to hide it but I didn't." The kid's voice cracked with remorse.

55

"I see." Mulligan nodded. "And you knew *why* she'd borrowed it? You knew she intended to use it *on him*?"

"Yes," the kid whispered. "He was mean. He beat us all the time and she told him not to do it any more."

Mulligan continued to ask the questions and the kid kept on answering them, believing he was helping clear his mother —until the big detective was satisfied he had the case wrapped up. Then he thanked the kid.

"And now you'll turn her loose and punish me instead?" the kid asked hopefully.

"Well," Mulligan hedged, "that's really not up to me." It was up to a judge and a jury. (Mulligan just asked the questions the way the D.A. expected them to be asked. He got the evidence the D.A. needed to convict. His methods were legal but he wasn't always proud of them. But, hell, it was a job—his job—and somebody had to do it, didn't they?)

"Oh," the kid said.

Just before he had left the juvenile hall, and after the kid had been returned to his quarters, Mulligan took a call from the coroner about the kid's old man.

"We just finished doing a routine post-mortem."

"So?"

"This guy had a brain tumor. This was practically a mercy death. He wouldn't've lived six months."

"I'll be damned!"

The judicial mills began to grind. The kid's mother was indicted for the homicide. Two and a half months later she went on trial. Defending her was an eager but inexperienced young lawyer appointed by the court.

The prosecutor's opening statement to the jury was terse and unemotional. "The People don't claim the deceased was a good man. They, in fact, concede he was a violent person of atrocious habits and despicable character. But that is beside the point. The sole question for you to decide, ladies and gentlemen of the jury, is whether, as we claim, the defendant here intentionally took the deceased's life in violation of the law of this state. We will establish by competent and convincing evidence that she did."

As his first witness, the prosecutor called the coroner. The corpus delicti—the proof and felonious means of death— was established. The revolver, marked at that point for identification only, was flashed dramatically before the jury. At the same time the prosecutor asked a seemingly innocent but explosive question. Yes, replied the coroner, he had examined the brain of the deceased. What had he found? A malignant tumor that would have caused death in a matter of months.

The young defense attorney bounded to his feet. "Your Honor, I move to strike the last two questions and answers on the ground they're incompetent, irrelevant, and immaterial."

"Motion granted," the trial judge stated.

"Very well," the prosecutor said, affecting a frown. Inwardly he was well pleased with himself. He'd put the case on the front pages, giving the newspaper boys an angle to play with, and he'd stampeded his green opponent into foreclosing himself from asking potentially embarrassing questions touching whether the tumor might have influenced the deceased's actions. His case was still nicely intact; he'd brought "his" jury to the edges of their chairs. What more could he ask? "Your witness, counsel," he said politely.

"No questions," the young lawyer shot back, satisfied he'd closed the door on any tricky maneuvering by the People's representative.

The prosecutor called the kid to the stand. Yes, the kid testified, he'd seen the gun before. Queried, he haltingly told where and under what circumstances. Instinctively the kid feared and mistrusted this man with the rapier intellect and smooth tongue. Too, the young attorney had warned him: "He'll try to prove motive and premeditation by your testimony." Then he carefully defined the key words. *I won't let him!* the kid told himself, parrying dangerously worded questions, evading entrapment, until, his patience worn thin, the prosecutor snatched up a document from the counsel table and demanded:

"Are these or are these not the questions asked you by Detective Lieutenant Mulligan and the answers given by you?"

They were, of course. And hearing his answers cold, when shock and numbing emotions no longer warped his thinking, here in the atmosphere of the courtroom, the kid realized with dread how fatal were those answers—but the truth—to his mother's cause. In trying to help her at a period when he had been altogether ignorant of the niceties, the technicalities, and the frigid impersonality of the law, he saw that he actually—and perhaps literally—had put a noose around her neck. He wanted then to shout it was a lie that the truth set free. It was as foolishly helpless against legalisms as it was against force.

"Well," the prosecutor snapped, "I'm waiting for an answer."

The kid turned to the judge in mute appeal. He was told, "You must answer the question." (Always the Authority figure was male; invariably it commanded that he act or speak against his will and conscience, and too often it sought to make him hurt or betray the female love object. This time, briefly, he rebelled.)

"I won't answer! You can't make me!"

But they did. They made him answer. A bailiff took a station beside the witness chair. The prosecutor stood over him, relentlessly waiting. The judge leaned toward him and curtly commanded him to answer or be held in contempt of court. They drew the answers from him and when he tried to qualify them, he was told to say only yes or no. Finally, in the midst of the interrogation, his mother stood up and said, "All right. If you want me to say it, I will. I'm guilty. *I'm guilty!* Now are you satisfied? Now will you stop torturing my son?"

After that the prosecutor was sympathetic, but he remaind deadly. He made sure his case was airtight. He left no loose ends. A tragic thing, he told the jury in his closing argument, a very tragic thing. But—and here he waved People's Exhibit One, the revolver—no one was given the right to take the law into his own hands. The defendant, he said, should have gone to the police; she had no legal justification for planning to take, and then taking, another human life, however vile. "Remember," he pontificated, referring to the brain tumor, "the Almighty in *His* infinite wisdom had already acted." There was a solemn nodding of heads in the jury box. The jury convicted the kid's mother of voluntary manslaughter and recommended leniency. The judge sentenced her to two years in the women's prison.

She was allowed a brief visit with her children before being transferred to the prison. The kid tried to be brave when his mother smiled and in a soft voice told him, "Be a good boy, Buddy. Trust in God, and look after Janey."

"I will, Mother," he said determinedly. "I promise I will." But when it was time to go he threw himself into his mother's arms and sobbed uncontrollably, scalding tears running down his cheeks. He had to be taken away forcibly by one of the attendants. At the door, he looked back.

On his mother's face was a look of torment, unendurable pain, black despair. The kid would never forget that look—and he would never see his mother again.

Chapter Ten

THE KID AND JANEY were wards of the court. After a perfunctory hearing, they were sent to an overcrowded, county-operated home where iron discipline took the place of love—or hate. Frightened and confused by the austerity of their new "home," its callousness, and wanting desperately to go to their mother, needing her, they ran off. But they didn't get far. Caught and returned, they were piously lectured and punished by being locked for five days in "meditation" rooms, where there were only cots and heavy mesh screens on the windows. Then they were moved to dormitories and kept separated.

"You two don't know how to act when you're together," the kid was told.

Janey had begun, alarmingly, to lose weight. While she never complained, she was found to be coughing up blood. Sputum tests indicated tuberculosis. X rays clinched the diagnosis: both lungs were badly involved. Hurriedly the red tape was cut through and she was sent to a sanitarium. "She won't last long," an attendant predicted. The words reached the kid. They made him shiver.

The kid received an even greater shock a few weeks later when he was called to the superintendent's office. "Your mother's dead," he was told. Just the fact, with no details, no offer of sympathy.

"No!" he protested. It couldn't be true. Yet it was. Far into the night he cried and prayed, and the other kids made fun of his tears and prayers, as they often had before. "Old cry baby's at it again," one of them said. The others snickered. His mother was dead. They didn't know and he wouldn't tell them. He wouldn't! His sobs grew louder. The night attendant told him to shut up. He did. He bottled up his feelings. The days passed; the nights.

And then the next thing he knew the Devil was standing at the foot of his bed.

60

"I thought it was about time I paid you another visit," the Devil said. "You don't seem to be doing so well."

"You're not real," the kid said. "Like last time, I'm just dreaming you're standing there."

"Believe what you will," the Devil replied indifferently. "My purpose in being here is not to dispute the matter of my reality with you."

"What do you want?"

A chuckle escaped the Devil's lips. "I believe the traditional reply would be that I want your soul."

"You fooled me once," the kid shouted. "I'm not going to let you do it again."

"Don't shout," the Devil admonished. "I have good ears. Now, precisely in what manner do you allege that I deceived you?"

"You know. You told me that nothing would happen to my mother if . . ." The kid couldn't bring himself to complete the sentence. He knew he was on dangerous ground.

"My little fool, I told you only what you wanted to hear."

"But . . ."

"Yes?"

"She's dead." There was awe and terror in the kid's choked voice. *His mother was dead.*

"I'm sorry," the Devil said. "But tears and prayers, or feeling sorry for yourself, can't change that."

"I loved her." His love and his need to love had been real, genuine. He had to make the Devil understand that. "Maybe I was scared of him, maybe I even secretly hated him, like you said, but I loved her."

"Granted. Now she's dead. Where does that leave you?"

"I don't know." It was best to be honest about that.

The Devil told him this time not what he wanted to hear, but what he had suspected as being the truth. There were times when you did have to be able to take it, when you stood up and hurled defiance into the teeth of the cosmos. Being free was what counted, free even of love if love were a smothering thing, an Achilles heel, if it brought only suffering and pain. Love for him was a screaming need, an addictive drug, and somehow, no matter how terrible the pains and delusions attending withdrawal, he had to free himself from all craving for it or in time it would surely destroy him.

That was what the Devil said, without fear of contradiction, and the kid felt himself impelled to agree. Present

61

was no heaven's advocate to challenge the validity of an argument that could only have had its origin in a hell of the mind, where torment shaded satanic, logical fallacies, and false premises won immediate acceptance with their hard, muscular promises of liberation—at a price.

I've got to be tough, the kid thought. *I've got to be strong. Nothing else matters.* He added, *Not now.*

"Correct," the Devil said, smiling with broad approval at the perception of this candidate. "And there's only one way."

"How?" the kid inquired eagerly.

"By letting hate and guile help you. With those two as your friends, you can take on the world. You won't know the meaning of fear."

The kid's mind was made up; his emotions were on fire. "I'll do it!"

"Fine," applauded the Devil, vastly pleased. "And in that case I guess I'll be getting along." There was, after all, such a thing as overselling the customer, whether you were plugging a new Cadillac or a berth in Hell.

"Will I see you again?"

The Devil's smile was enigmatic. "Well, I rather doubt it. I believe from here on you'll make out splendidly without any further assistance or advice from me."

With those sardonic words, the Devil disappeared. The kid would never "see" him again. But often thereafter the Devil's mocking laughter would ring in his ears.

When you rebel against a tyrant, real or imagined, you must strike swiftly if you hope to succeed, first making certain that no avenue of retreat is left open. Too, when the tyrant's name is Love and has a terrible protector named Fear, you must have satisfied yourself of the unswerving fealty of the warriors serving you, Hate and Guile. Otherwise there is danger that your insurrection will be aborted, and you again will find yourself the slave-prisoner of this tyrannical master against whom you rose, your chains and the walls of your dungeon prison more secure than ever, more agonizingly painful.

The kid found a way to condition himself for, and irrevocably commit himself to, the rebellion to come, as well as to burn the only bridge that would let him flee back to the tormenting safety of his bondage should he panic, when a rodent-faced boy, called the Rat by the other youngsters at the home, stopped him one day.

"Let's be friends, huh?" the Rat said.

The kid knew that the Rat was despised by the other boys because he was a double-crosser, a stoolie, a bootlicker. That, not his physical appearance, accounted for his nickname.

"Friends?" Friends with a snake, a fink, a phony? "Sure," the kid said. "Why not?" Wasn't this a sure-fire way to get the other guys to be suspicious of him, to earn their mistrust, to become ostracized? And wouldn't that in turn justify his dislike of them? Wouldn't it help him to stand alone and apart by choice? He thought: *I won't give a damn what they think.*

The kid and the Rat became pals. It was a strange relationship, one that put curious demands upon the latter, that necessitated his constantly rationalizing his conduct. He'd say, his shifty beady eyes pleading for assurance, "You know, don't you, Buddy, that I only took"—he'd never use the word "steal"—"those candy bars from Jimmy because he'd borrowed some from me and wouldn't pay me back?" Or "The only reason I told Mr. Aimes the truth about what Frankie did is because he was trying to get us all in trouble. You knew that, didn't you?"

It was then that the kid began to grin. "Hell," he'd say, recalling that his old man often prefaced his remarks with casual reference to the infernal regions, "anything you do's okay with me."

"And we're still buddies?"

"Till the end."

But the Rat was never satisfied. When the kid would grin, a secret doubt would stab at him. *Maybe he's laughing at me!* the Rat would think. But the kid was his pal, the first one he'd ever had. Or was he, really? He'd ask, again and again, getting repeated assurances. Still, his doubt grew until in time it became certainty: *He's not my buddy at all; he's just pretending he is for some reason. That makes him worse than all the rest of them combined. I'll make him sorry he did this to me. I'll get even with him.*

And even as the Rat prepared to betray the kid, he won yet another assurance that they still were friends, and he trembled at the possibility he was making a mistake. But his loveless, twisted mind drove him to plant the stolen money and wallet, taken from one of the attendants, in the kid's

63

locker and then to go to the head attendant. "I know where Mr. Blake's wallet and money are," he said.

"Where?"

"In Buddy's locker. I saw him put it there, and he told me he swiped the stuff."

The kid was perversely pleased with this betrayal. He took bitter pleasure in the corporal punishment and the thirty-day lockup in the meditation room. He grinned at the fact that the framed-up charge won him the enmity of authority and, further, that his betrayer, who had betrayed himself as well, went unpunished and was even rewarded. When they tried to get him to tell why he had stolen the wallet and money, he simply refused to say a word. He declined to so much as deny the charge or protest his innocence. He elected, rather, to grin at them all and to forge from the incident the armor he would wear when his rebellion was open and declared. That would be soon, very soon.

Released from the meditation room with a pious lecture and an ill-humored warning that if he was in any more trouble he would be sent to juvenile court and dealt with severely, he was returned to his dormitory. He waited, biding his time. Then, when the opportunity presented itself, grinning, he assaulted and seriously injured the Rat with an iron bar. It was an act committed without passion. Taken before the head attendant, he stubbornly refused to express remorse. "I'm not sorry I did it," he told his angry inquisitors. When they pressed him, he shouted defiantly, "I'm glad!"

He was—for now there could be no turning back. The papers were quickly drawn up declaring him to be an incorrigible unfit for the home: thief, a liar, a constitutional inadequate, a defier of authority, in short, a young John Dillinger, if the report were to be believed (and it of course would be accepted as gospel). This time it wasn't juvenile hall for him but the juvenile tank at the county jail. There he was held while his case was being processed and until it could be heard. As overcrowded as the home, the tank—a line of thirteen cells fronted by a walkway—was jammed with boys between the ages of fourteen and seventeen, dull ones and smart ones, fledgling psychopaths and timid truants, the crafty and the cornered.

The kid was educated fast. Four youthful toughs, assigned to the Nos. 1 and 2 cells, bossed the tank. For doing so, and keeping down trouble, they were granted small favors by the old jailer in charge. For example, he winked at the kangaroo court they conducted and looked the other way when they ran a crap game in a back cell, using dice made of soap.

"Fish on the line," somebody yelled when the kid was passed into the tank. The head trusty told the kid he'd be sleeping on the floor—they were overcrowded—in the No. 9 cell until seniority got him a bunk. "Or if you got a buck, I'll throw somebody out of theirs now and give it to you."

The kid didn't have any money.

"Christ," the trusty said, "I suppose the next thing you'll tell me is that you're not here for stealing."

"That's right," a skinny gunsel jeered. "I hear he raped a pig and it squealed on him." His laughed was like a seal's bark.

"Dummy up, punk," the husky young head trusty said. "And take a hike."

The gunsel slunk off.

"What're you in for?"

"I hit a guy with an iron bar at the orphanage."

"How come?"

"He said I'd stolen the attendant's wallet. Now I guess they'll send me to reform school but I don't care."

"You lookin' for a rep maybe?"

"A what?"

"A reputation," the trusty said impatiently, all the time appraising the kid, asking himself the relevant questions: Can he be pushed around? Or turned out (as a passive partner in homosexual acts)? Is he a solid guy or a fink?

Here, the kid immediately perceived, a tough front and an ability and hair-trigger willingness to use your dukes paid off. Here, too, the pecking order was quickly established. And here the heroes weren't baseball, boxing, or other sports greats; they were bank robbers and killers.

"I'm just looking to get along," the kid said.

"Sure," the head trusty said. Then he called to all the others in the tank and convened the kangaroo court. He was the judge and the No. 2 trusty was the prosecutor. The kid was charged with breaking into jail. Before they could give him his sentence it was time for evening chow and the cell doors were racked and then sprung one at a time. The youngsters lined up for their stew, slaw, and bread pudding in the order in which they were assigned to their cells. The guys who belonged behind the kid began to crowd in front of him and one of them growled, "Don't you like it?"

65

They were testing him, as they did every newcomer. And if he let them walk over him now he would be lost. He'd end up a whipped cur or somebody's brat. He had to declare himself and he had to do it in a language they would understand.

He held out his metal plate for his serving of stew and slaw. The head trusty, who was dishing out the stew, pushed two big pieces of meat off the ladle and gave him only juice and vegetables.

"How come I don't get any meat?" the kid asked.

"Because I don't feel like giving you any," the head trusty said. "Think that's a good enough reason?"

The kid grinned. He snatched up the stew bucket and slammed it in the head trusty's face. "No," he said. "I don't think that's a good enough reason." Then he took a murderous swipe at the No. 2 trusty, who leaped back out of range, and added, "Are there any more of you smart sonofabitches that want trouble?"

There weren't.

The old jailer threw the kid in the hole and left him there, shivering with the cold, for three days and nights. Each day he tried to get the kid to say he wouldn't cause any more trouble if he let him out. The kid refused. His hostility toward authority grew. The night screw wanted to slip him some blankets but the kid told him to shove them. "I don't want anything from you people," he said.

By the time he was returned to the tank, the youngsters it held had convinced themselves the kid was crazy, a dangerous, unpredictable nut, and they were willing to leave him strictly alone, which was the way he wanted it. "You can't trust anybody!" had become the kid's motto. He'd "proved" it. The festering sickness in his soul went undetected.

Finally he had his juvenile court hearing. The judge handling the case, an old, wizened, and austere personage, embraced some remarkable views on heredity. Reviewing the family history—the father "a drunken, brawling, irresponsible ex-pugilist"; the mother an "unstable husband-slayer"—his Honor concluded that the kid was tainted, that is, genetically or constitutionally disposed to violence and consequently a menace to society. Ergo, the kid needed large doses of discipline and "training."

Judgment followed the solemn mouthing of this medieval, syllogistic nonsense: a commitment to reform school.

The following day, handcuffed, his legs shackled, the kid was driven to the school. His newly acquired reputation for incorrigibility and violence went with him. So did the wall of rebellious defiance he had built around himself. It was at this correctional institution, so called, that he learned to use his hands to hold off the world and to smash it back. The milieu was a savage one, with emphasis placed on regimentation, on rigid conformity or else. The front office talk of "rehabilitation" was a joke. Fear and coercion, punishment and the threat of punishment didn't socialize, and never would.

The superintendent was a figurehead, a bumbling character who made speeches to women's groups on the fine work being done at his institution but who didn't know what was going on. The chief disciplinary and job officer, "Whispering Annie," the inmates and personnel alike called him, was the real boss, and he was a boss with an iron hand. He interviewed all new arrivals and laid down the law in a hoarse whisper. To "Whispering Annie" it was, of course, an unqualified "truth" that society was entirely "right" and the rebel wholly "wrong." Accordingly, whatever the rebel's background, his intelligence and educational level, his personality, his race and the social and economic status of his family, it was, in "Whispering Annie's" opinion, the school's function to make the rebel fit a Procrustean bed of "good citizenship," which meant submissive acceptance of and blind obedience to authority. "Whispering Annie's" authority, the school's authority—an absolutist authority. Under such conditions "straightening out" meant defeat, a kind of behavioral gelding.

"You think you're a tough guy," "Whispering Annie" told the kid at the outset of their initial encounter. "But I don't. I've never met a real tough guy on your side of the fence. So you better fly right. You cause us any real trouble and we'll break you."

"That's your job," the kid said, grinning.

"You don't fool me. Remember that. Now get out of here and keep your nose clean."

The kid got out. His indoctrination was underway. He learned in rapid order about toilet lines and guard lines. Assigned first to a receiving company for younger boys, he soon found himself standing stiffly at attention with five other youngsters beside the Man's raised platform in quarters. They were all being punished because somebody at his table had broken the silence rule by whispering. The boy next to the kid began to squirm. "I gotta go to the toilet," he whined.

"Shut up," the Man snapped. "It's a half-hour to line time."

The boy continued to squirm. "I can't wait."

One of the Man's three monitors (inmates selected to help him run the company) stepped up behind the boy and struck him viciously in the kidney area. "Get up to attention and go on the dummy!" The boy fell to the floor, moaning and urinating.

Again the kid found himself under compulsion to act. He spun around and spit in the monitor's face. The other two monitors came on the run from the locker room. All three of them handed the kid a bad drubbing but he took it grinning and didn't back up an inch. A wild swing knocked a monitor halfway across the room before the Man stepped in and broke it up. "All right," he said. "All right. That's enough. Don't mark him up too bad."

The kid's mind sang a hymn of hate as he was hustled to the segregated disciplinary company. As they threw him into a cell, he laughed. (He laughed even louder and more sardonically when he learned later that the whiner, on whose behalf he had intervened, had become the punk of the monitor who had belted him. That was the way it went in this fenced-in jungle.) The kid had made two all-important discoveries. He could hit with either hand and somewhere he had jettisoned his almost paralyzing fear of being physically hurt. In place of the fear was a wild, atavistic joy of battle.

"Whispering Annie" ordered the "water cure" for him the next morning. They stripped him and played a powerful stream of water from a fire hose on him. He laughed at them and he hardened. It became a personal battle of wills between him and "Annie." He took what they had to offer in the way of "discipline": unpalatable light rations, cold-water hosings, the hole for long stretches, floggings. He didn't break; he fought back, grinning, sustained by hate.

Butch was sent to the school. The kid heard about his arrival and stayed out of trouble long enough to win his release from the disciplinary unit. Then he looked up Butch in the gym. "Well," the kid grinned, "what took you so long to get here, you would-be double-tough sonofabitch?"

Butch had heard frightening stories about the kid, how he'd turned hard and wild and crazy. He offered his hand, smiling in a sickly way, more than ready to be friends. But the kid ignored the proffered hand. Quietly he told Butch off. He made him admit he wasn't tough. Figuratively he made him

68

crawl. "Even your name ain't original," the kid said. "It's as phony as you are."

Butch played it safe. He acted surprised and hurt. What had happened between them before was ancient history. "Jeez," he added, "guys from the same district oughtta stick together. They're supposed to be buddies."

"Buddies chase rabbits and eat shit," the kid said, repeating the vulgar philosophism that only fools had friends. He walked off.

The institution was divided into two sections. On one side was the "reform school" for those fifteen to eighteen years of age; on the other, the "reformatory" for those eighteen to twenty-one. Before being released on an automatic parole, the kid had spent many rugged months in segregation on the reformatory side.

Chapter Eleven

THE KID'S SISTER, Janey, hadn't died, although twice she almost had. Nor, while she had rallied, was she yet well. She remained at the sanitarium, waging an uncomplaining battle for her life. The kid's first act, following his release from the reformatory, was to go to see her. He went even before he had reported to his parole officer.

They looked at one another, almost as strangers, and saw immediately the profound change in each other. Janey was thin, fragile, wasted, with an ethereal beauty and a quiet faith in God and her fellows that shone from her clear gray eyes. The kid, contrastingly, had grown tall and muscular; his gray-green eyes were frighteningly cold, his face was a battered, grinning mask. And he then had no God, no faith in anyone or anything except his ability to hold off the world with his fists. He was too plainly a hard young tough.

"Oh, Buddy!" Janey cried, "what have they done to you?"

Janey had always called him Buddy. So had his mother, the kid recalled bitterly. And so had the Rat.

"They've wised me up," he said, using the reform school expression. "They dried me off behind the ears and taught me the score."

They talked, this young brother and sister who now were so different, and their talk took them back to the past, for it was the past, and its wrenching cruelty, that they had in common. Because it had to be done, it was like walking in a mine field, knowingly. And, inevitably, the mine was struck; the mine within, waiting only to be triggered. From Janey the kid learned that their mother had not died of a disease or from an accident—*she had committed suicide!*

She had hanged herself in the dark grimness of an isolation cell. He had never known.

The implosion that took place within the kid was soundless but its shock waves shook and racked his body; they momentarily stripped the mask from his face. Briefly they made him human again, and vulnerable.

He wanted to cry but he had forgotten how. He knew only how to hate. He perceived in that moment of anguish that a fierce and flaming capacity to hate, particularly when it was directed somehow against his old man, was all he had left. He felt maddeningly impotent because he couldn't bring the murdered dead man back to life and kill him all over again, slowly. Still, neither could he forget the frenzied words his terrible old man had shouted when beating him:

"You gotta be able to take it! Goddamn it, do you hear me? You gotta be able to take it!"

You first had to be able to take everything the world, or the guy you were fighting, could dish out; then you had to fight back, letting that awful hatred erupt and burst out of you.

When you couldn't take it any more you were through.

And when you couldn't dish it out any more you were through.

Once you took off the rose-colored glasses, kicked aside all the fancy window dressing, and smashed through the illusions that otherwise would keep you from seeing the raw and naked truth, however ugly and repelling it might be, you got smart to the fact that this was a world of treacherous carnivorous jungle bipeds, not men—and the kid despised it. Everything about it.

He despised it and was tormented by it. Some of the reasons he knew; others were buried. They were the assassins of rationality and they stalked about in the dark, unseen. This much was certain: his mother and his old man were dead, Janey might be dying, and he—well, he laughed sardonically and told himself he didn't give a damn. *I'm no good*, he thought; which, if true, would have left him with no problem at all. The hell of it was that, undeniably, he was *some* good, some small, indestructible fraction good.

And, as a result, the kid could neither possess his soul nor lose it; he could only slowly destroy himself as love and hate drove him relentlessly in opposite directions. At one pole was the memory of his mother and what she had taught him of God and love and goodness, even order and centrality, purpose and peace. At the other pole was the memory of his old man, the bullying nihilist, and his sneering rejection of all values except the most savagely primitive and doubtful

71

ones—you might say the "values" of mockery, of crudity, of bellicosity.

Looking back, later, he would recall little of what he and Janey had said after he had learned about their mother's suicide. For the assassins were at work.

"Come in," the man behind the desk called out curtly. A bureaucrat to the core of him, he didn't look up but continued to leaf importantly through a thick sheaf of papers.

The kid entered and stood in front of the desk, waiting to be acknowledged. He glanced incuriously first at the man and then, briefly, at the office. The man was not tall, judging from what the kid could see of him, and he had a flat face, narrow shoulders, and an abnormally large head. The nameplate on the desk declared the man's name to be A. J. Warden.

Isn't this a helluva note, the kid thought. *The comedian's going to be my parole officer and his name's Warden. Well, it looks like the little bastard's got a face and personality to match his name.*

Warden, thrusting aside the thick sheaf of papers, looked up suddenly. His pale blue eyes were as cold as the kid's. "Well," he snapped, "where's your 2-B-3 form? Let me have it! I haven't all day."

"You mean this?" the kid asked, holding up the arrival form the receptionist in the outer office had given him to complete.

"Of course I mean that," Warden said with the controlled exasperation he obviously reserved for the young parolees in his charge. In his estimation they were an impertinent, undisciplined lot who almost invariably needed to be put in line promptly. Show them who's boss, was Warden's authoritarian philosophy. Use the big verbal stick. Make them toe the line.

Warden snatched the form from the kid and studied it. "You're late." The words were, somehow, more than a bare statement of fact. They exceeded accusation, being plainly intended to intimidate.

The kid grinned. "A day late," he conceded.

Warden came to his feet. A redness began to climb up his neck. "And you appear to be of the opinion that being late is ground for levity."

"If you mean I think it's funny, I don't, exactly. I just don't think that it's cause to get your bowels in an uproar about."

Warden fairly ran around his desk. "It isn't what you think. It's what *I* think! Understand that! Get it through your thick

72

head!" He shook his stubby right index finger in the kid's still grinning face. His neck was swelling, like a toad's. He was something out of *Alice in Wonderland*, improbable but real—and dangerous.

"When the reformatory officials instructed you to report here yesterday morning, you were expected to do just that. Apparently you don't realize that parole is a privilege, not a right. You still have some three years to serve and you'll do well to keep in mind that it's within my power to return you at any time." Warden was breathing hard and trying to stare the kid down. He subsided, waiting for the full coercive impact of his words to register on this grinning young fool and, figuratively, to drive him to his knees, mouthing apologies.

"I know all that," the kid said, unimpressed.

The grin goaded Warden to new heights of outraged fury. How dare this insolent idiot laugh at him? By God, he would teach this one a lesson he wouldn't ever forget! He lashed at him with his tongue. He told him about another "swaggering punk" who thought he was bigger than society and its laws and who, as an inevitable consequence (by authoritarian logic), ended up being fried in the electric chair. He painted with a bold verbal brush other bloodcurdling pictures of a crime-doesn't-pay nature. Only by a passive acceptance of authority and its mandates could redemption be won, he perorated.

And then the kid did laugh. Little did this self-important, long-winded, flat-faced little bastard know. You had to be able to take it. You didn't let authority con you or break you. You died before you whined or crawled on your belly. And when the going got tough, you could always depend on hate and guile to give you a hand. All that you'd learned at the reformatory. You'd taken the best they had to offer and now here was some phony, weight-throwing parole officer trying to bulldoze you into kissing his ass. And he was so dense it didn't occur to him that all you wanted to do was kick that particular part of his anatomy.

"You can save the sermon," the kid said. "It leaves me cold."

At this heresy Warden's eyes literally bugged in their sockets. "Why . . . why," he spluttered, beside himself with indignation. "How dare you speak to *me* like that?"

"Warden," the kid said softly, "it's sonofabitches like you

73

that convince guys like me society is something we want no part of."

"Oh ho!" shouted Warden. "So you admit it. You admit you're antisocial. They should never have let you out in the first place. You're not fit to live in the society of decent human beings! Well, if the school hasn't sense enough to protect society from the likes of you, I have. I'm violating your parole right here and now."

"Good for you," the kid said. The grin hadn't left his face but now there was something frightening about it and his eyes glittered dangerously. A more prudent man than A. J. Warden would have taken heed.

"What sort of mother could have raised such a worthless and vicious son?" Warden demanded rhetorically.

The kid's left hand slammed into the parole officer's flabby stomach and the air whooshed out of him. An instant later, before he could fall, the kid backhanded him across the face. Warden sprawled across his desk. He incontinently emptied the contents of his assaulted belly onto the thick sheaf of papers. Too ill to rise or speak, he lay there and groaned.

The frilly young receptionist dashed into the office, looked, gasped, and asked excitedly, "What in the world happened to Mr. Warden?"

"Mr. Warden," the kid said with unmistakable satisfaction, "had an accident." Then he walked out.

He returned to his old district. It had changed. Or was it he who had changed? Both, probably. For time allowed nothing to remain the same. He remembered the beer joint where his old man had made him take a drink and smoke a cigarette. It was still there but there was a new face behind the bar. Well, now was as good a time as any to erase his humiliation. He planted himself on one of the bar stools and ordered a Coke.

"You mean a Coke high?"

"No, I mean just what I said. A Coke, period."

The bartender shrugged. "Comin' up."

A redhead with a saucy face, seated on his left, turned to him and said, "I saw that happen in the movies once."

"Yeah," the kid replied, "so did I. Only the guy ordered milk. I should've, too."

"Why?"

"Because I was looking for trouble. I wanted somebody

74

not to like it so I could knock his goddamned teeth down his throat."

"Why?"

"You a cop or you writing a book?"

The redhead laughed gaily. "Neither," she said. "I'm a nymphomaniac named Frankie who aspires to be a famous artist. Would you care to visit my apartment and see my etchings?"

"You're a smart dame."

"On the contrary, I'm an honest dame. Come on, I'll show you." She took the kid gently but firmly by the arm, impelled him out the door and guided him to an expensive, late-model convertible. She drove across town as though pursued by the devil himself. She lived in the bohemian quarter that was mostly a tourist trap. He had to run to keep up as she ascended the creaky stairs to her attic apartment. After turning on the lights she swept the airy room with her hand and said, "You see."

Hr frowned and scratched his head at the paintings lining the walls.

"I thought so," she laughed. "You're a square."

He was surprised by her use of the expression. "Me?" he said. "A square don't do a lot of time in a reformatory and then belt his parole officer soon as he gets out."

"And now they're after you."

"Yeah. I owe 'em three years."

"What are you going to do?"

"I don't know."

"You can stay here until you make up your mind. Unless, that is, you're afraid of me."

"Why should I be afraid of you?"

"You'll find out."

She was a rebel, too. Just as he had rebelled against authority, she had rebelled against convention. She lived as she pleased, she said, and to prove it she seduced him. In doing so, she doubtless saved him from being shot dead or executed. For, corroded by hate, driven by a need to prove he could do without everything they said made life worth living, he had been ready to turn to crime, to become a mad dog and declare a war on authority, not surreptitiously but brazenly, defiantly, violently. Consequently, he had been grateful for the authoritarian Warden. A decent, thoughtful guy would have made it tough to justify open criminal warfare. But Warden made it easy. Bastards like him always did. Only now there was a new factor, casually introduced but decisive: "a nymphomaniac named Frankie," an unconventionalist, a cubist. He didn't understand her art but he did learn from it and her that only an idiot could be goaded to do the expected, the conventional. So crime was out. A week after they met, and after a week of sexual giving and taking, but never sharing, the kid had this saucy-faced redhead drive him out to the reformatory. They shook hands and said "So long" unemotionally—for good.

The kid flattened out his three years the hard way, rebelliously, spending most of it in solitary or the hole. When he walked out the front gate the next time he had paid his debt in full. He had reached his majority and he and the state were quits. That was the way he wanted it.

Chapter Twelve

IT WAS KNOWN as Chosen, which meant "morning calm," and there, legend has it, a dynasty was founded some eleven hundred years before the birth of Christ. In black headlines almost two thousand years after the crucifixion of the gentle Nazarene, it would be called Korea. On June 25, 1950, this divided and strife-ridden nation of 85,000 square miles became an international incident and then, a few days later, an international battleground.

That Sunday morning, shattering the "morning calm," North Korean Communist troops smashed across the 38th parallel into the U.N.-recognized Republic of South Korea. Their avowed goal: by force of arms to put all of this 600-mile-long peninsula that jutted out from Asia between the Yellow Sea and the Sea of Japan under the domination of the North Korean People's Republic. They very nearly succeeded.

On June 27, 1950, two days after the invasion had been launched, President Harry Truman ordered armed intervention by the military of the United States. That same Tuesday, military sanctions were invoked against North Korea by the United Nations. The next day the Reds captured Seoul, and on July 1 a battalion of the United States 24th Infantry Division was flown to Korea. In a matter of days, almost hours, U.S. troops engaged the enemy, fighting a heroic delaying action with the South Koreans, and General Douglas MacArthur was named Supreme Commander for the United Nations by President Truman.

On a hot July day, in a large American city, a tall, cold-eyed young man heard a newsboy shout that the small American forces, along with the South Korean troops, were being swept down the Chosen peninsula. If the impetus of the attack could be sustained, they would be hurled into the sea.

The young man invested seven cents in a newspaper. He

77

stood on a busy street corner and read of the violence that had boiled up half a world away. He looked at the maps with their strange names: Pyongyang, Seoul, Pusan. He examined the pictures, showing bewildered children, gutted buildings, uniformed men fighting and dying.

What struck this young man was how uncomplicated it was, how beautifully and violently black and white. The rules were so damned few and so elemental, too. It was a big, savage scrap, and it was possible for him to be a part of it. That was what he liked most. Hell, it was almost as though they had started the conflict just to accommodate him. He was grateful to them, all of them: the Soviets, the North Koreans, and later the Chinese Reds; the ideological big domes, the fanatics, the power hungry, and even (or especially) his opposite numbers, the guys like himself on the other side who would be trying to kill him while he was trying to kill them.

This young man had no difficulty locating the nearest recruiting station of the United States Army and when he was handed a form to fill out he felt confident it would be only a matter of time—and not too much time—before he, a soldier of the United States, would be shipped to the war zone. It didn't work out this way, however. His timetable was knocked into a cocked hat and almost his entire plan. The first hint of trouble came when he encountered the question on the form: "Have you ever been arrested?"

He of course had, for he was the kid—the kid with a past and two trips to the reformatory. The Army at first didn't want him but he talked his way in. "What do you want," he told the army psychiatrist, "a guy that's willing and knows how to fight or some scared little mama's boy?" He was unaware of the irony of his words. The psychiatrist undoubtedly wasn't.

Stateside, the kid didn't make a very good soldier. He was slow to accept the discipline, the barked commands of the big, beefy sergeant who had charge of the rookies at the training division where the kid was first sent. He had no love for authority in any form and it galled him to submit himself to the regimen but he needed an enemy, so he adjusted after a fashion and held back his hate, letting it build up in him. He did his latrine and K.P. duty with a grin. He got himself tossed into the guardhouse and still he grinned. He told himself it wouldn't be too long before he would have his chance to play murderously and for keeps. So this wasn't too big a price to pay.

The weeks passed. United States and South Korean forces had held on doggedly to a 4,000 square mile beachhead in southeast Korea. On September 15, under General Mac-Arthur, the United States 10th Corps made an amphibious landing at Inchon. Before the month was out Seoul was recaptured. A few days later United Nations forces crossed the 38th parallel into North Korea. On October 14, President Truman and General MacArthur met on Wake Island. Pyongyang, capital of North Korea, was captured on October 19. United Nations forces were on the march to the Yalu.

Then, on October 25, the Red Chinese Army intervened. Hundreds of thousands of troops came swarming across the Yalu from Manchuria into North Korea. A month later, after both the forces of South Korea and the United States had reached the Manchurian border, the Chinese launched a massive offensive. Under the impact, the U.N. troops reeled back. Soon they would be forced to abandon Pyongyang.

By now, the kid had been shipped with an outfit to Japan. There he and the others were toughened for what lay ahead by being run up and down Nipponese mountains under simulated battle conditions. The kid's patience was wearing thin. His temper was hair-trigger quick. The U.S. Army had made him into a soldier, it had taught him to handle weapons and kill and dodge death and do all those things a front-line doughfoot is expected to do, and now it seemed that that same Army was perversely holding him back.

"What the hell are we waiting for?" the kid repeatedly demanded. "If they keep stalling much longer, the damn' war'll be lost before we get a chance to get to it even."

"You wait right here, soldier," a noncom once shot back sarcastically. "The general and his staff oughta know that. Sometimes they have a real hard time running a show like this without help from military geniuses like you that've been in this man's army a whole ninety days."

Some of the kid's frustration and anger dissipated itself when he had a picture of himself telling the big brass what to do. Jeez, what a farce that would be!

Grinning, he told the noncom, "Kiss my tokus."

"I would," the noncom replied, "but it looks too much like your face."

"Big joke."

The kid's outfit was transferred to Korea in December,

when the U.N. forces, trapped at the Changjin Reservoir, were battling to escape. By the day before Christmas they had succeeded, with heavy casualties. From Hungnam they were evacuated by sea.

Lieut. Gen. Walton H. Walker was killed at the front in a jeep accident. Command of the U.S. Eighth Army, of which the kid's outfit was a part, was taken over by Lieut. Gen. Matthew B. Ridgway. The U.N. troops were in retreat. The new year was only four days old when the Reds recaptured Seoul.

"Looks like we got here just in time," the kid told a scared eighteen-year-old in his company.

"It sure does," the youngster agreed mournfully. "Just in time to get ourselves killed awful dead."

The kid patted his automatic rifle affectionately and grinned. "I bet I get me just a whole lot of gooks and heathen Chinee before that happens."

On January 25 the U.N. forces determinedly returned to the offensive. The kid was part of this new drive north, part of the war machine that was smashing its way back up to the 38th parallel. He froze and cursed and marched and fought through February and into March, when Seoul, abandoned by the Reds without a fight, was reoccupied.

"Now the bastards are trying to run us to death," he beefed, just before a sniper's whining bullet sent him diving for cover. Mouthing obscenities, the kid rolled behind a wall, then in a flash was on his feet and, running in a crouch, began stalking his man. In a reckless way, by exposing himself and drawing the other's fire, he got his man. Laughing and on the run, he shot him off the top of a fire-ravaged building. He shot him again when he hit the ground.

His suicidal act won him an on-the-spot chewing out by the looie over him. "You crazy?" the looie shouted. "No, don't answer that. You've got to be crazy. Dammit, I've told you a dozen times before and now I'm telling you for the last time. *Stop the grandstanding!*"

"Look," the kid said, "I wasn't grandstanding. And don't ask me again if I'm trying to get myself shipped back home in a box with some cotton in my ass and a medal around my neck. I'm not and you should know it."

The looie threw up his hands in despair. "I don't know what to think. I keep telling you not to take wild chances but you won't listen. You act like you think you've got to win this war all by yourself."

"I can't figure you people out," the kid rejoined. "You bring me over here to fight. You tell me how tough and cunning these characters we're fighting are. *We* gotta be tough, you tell us. We gotta fight like hell. So okay. That suits me fine. I try to fight like you want me to. Then I get a big growl from you for doing what you told me to do in the first place."

"Stop it!" the looie said. "Can it or you'll have me convinced I'm a heel for trying to keep you in one piece."

"I don't need a nursemaid, Loot."

Later the lieutenant asked the captain, "What do you do with a toughie like that?"

"I would say," the captain ventured, "that you see he's aimed in the right direction and kept well supplied with ammunition."

So the kid found his requests for the most dangerous patrols granted. Repeatedly, until he was ready to drop from exhaustion, he gladly went out on missions that he converted into virtual suicide assignments—and always, miraculously, he returned with a whole skin and a grin on his scraggly bearded face that would have frightened the devil himself.

"This," he exulted, "is more like it." He had put his hate to work. He lived for the moment alone, for each squeeze of the trigger, each pull of a grenade pin. Fighting and killing, he never looked back—or ahead, except in fierce anticipation of what additional danger and violence tomorrow might hold. This in truth and in fact was the perfect milieu of the psychopath whose pathology didn't let him know fear. Its savagery satisfied the kid wholly.

The frigid Korean winter gave way grudgingly to a wet Korean spring. A United States tank patrol sliced across the 38th parallel. . . .

Word got around. "We're moving out in the morning. Something big's coming up."

A new northward drive got underway. Pushing hard, the kid's outfit slogged its way through mud that at times was like sticky glue. But for miles it could locate no enemy. It was almost as though this enemy literally had been swallowed up by the accursed rain-soaked earth beneath and around them.

"Maybe they quit and went home," one of the kid's buddies joked, with a wistful note in his voice. "They heard we were coming and they figured they didn't have a chance."

"Ain't you the dreamer," the kid said. He added grimly, "It's probably some kind of a trick."

It was.

At dawn the kid's company found itself the target of a bugle-blowing, can-beating, screaming enemy surprise attack. The Reds, seemingly materializing from nowhere, charged from three sides, forcing them back into a pocket. They beat off the first three waves of troops thrown at them but knew they wouldn't be able to hold out very long.

It was the first and last time the kid told the United States Army what to do and got away with it. "Captain," he said during a lull, "most of you people can get out of this goddamned trap if you leave some of us behind."

"I'm quite aware of that, soldier."

"Then what the hell are you waiting for? I'm your first volunteer. Start finding out who else wants to stay behind and fight."

The captain's jaw clamped shut. He looked coldly at the grinning, murderous doughfoot who should have got himself killed weeks earlier. Then his eyes flicked around at the others crouched down near him. Seconds before, they had been hit by the last wave. Seconds away was a fourth screaming wave, now forming, ready to hurl itself forward. The captain saw his own dead and wounded, and the enemy's. He knew the Reds cared nothing for casualties or human life if they could realize their military objectives. It was hardly a time for him to be hesitating or worrying about the insolence of a young private who had just demanded the dubious "privilege" of suicidally covering the retreat of the remainder of the company.

Quickly the captain gave the word. He wanted volunteers. He got them, nineteen of them. There were more than twice that many but that was all he accepted.

The kid was a walking arsenal when, seconds later, he saluted the captain, a mocking glint in his eyes and a diabolical grin across his lean face. He's snatched up all the ammo and grenades he could pack. "Cap," he said, "it looks like this one time I'm going to get to do all the fighting I want the way I want without getting chewed out by your baby sitters. So when we hit 'em, you people show me how fast you can run, will you?"

A tough, hard-boiled cookie himself, who had fought his way through Europe during World War II, the captain grinned back at the kid. "Soldier, if I ever see you again, depend on me to do three things."

"What are they?"

"First I'm going to shake your hand; second, see that you get a medal for bravery . . ."

"And third?"

"Third, this number ten and a half here, I'm going to plant in your gluteal region with much pleasure."

When the next wave of enemy troops began its assault, the nineteen volunteers moved out to meet them, machine guns blazing. The audacity probably more than the impact of this sudden counterattack, for such the enemy thought it to be, broke the forward motion of the attack. Momentarily the Reds found themselves in the role of defenders when, seconds previously, they had been on the offensive, with everything going their way. They re-formed and concentrated on crushing a breakthrough. While on its hands and knees, often on its belly, the company crept silently to freedom (northward, later doubling back), the nineteen absorbed the enemy's full fury while slashing southward.

The second lieutenant in charge was the first to get it. Next was the eighteen-year-old, the frightened youngster who had fought down his fear to volunteer for a mission he had known to be suicidal, and, with his face blown almost away, whose prediction had come true: he was "awful dead." Soon the nineteen were only nine. Then eight. Seven. Six.

And the kid became a demon from hell. He hurled grenades and obscenities. He fired hot-barreled weapons snatched from wounded, dying, and dead members of the volunteer unit. It was only seconds more until he saw with blood-reddened eyes that he was the only man left standing. Then the enemy was upon him. He met them with a trench knife and was shot at point-blank range. He collapsed.

Writhing on the ground, trying to pull the pin from a grenade, he was shot again. Shot, too, and killed, methodically murdered, were four wounded volunteers. But he wasn't dead; later he said that he didn't have sense enough to die. Cursing, he got to his feet with a superhuman effort and grinned hideously at his captors. They were amazed he was still alive; so was he. He amazed them and himself even more by remaining on his feet, although reeling drunkenly, all the way to a cleverly camouflaged field GHQ of the enemy for this sector. There, swaying dizzily, with the most tenuous grip on consciousness, the kid was questioned by a Chinese major through a buck-toothed interpreter. The interrogation was really more of a political harangue than anything. What was he doing in Korea? What the hell did they think he was doing! Playing tiddlywinks, maybe?

Besides, how stupid could you get? What was the percentage in putting on a show for a bleeding, shot-up doughfoot who thought he was dying and who couldn't even be sure he knew how to spell ideology, let alone discuss competing ones. "So, all right," he said sarcastically, calling on the last of his strength. "You're all a bunch of humanitarians that want to save the world from some potbellied characters on Wall Street, and my name's Napoleon Bonaparte. Now where do we go from there?"

The interpreter—"gopher mouth," the kid called him—tapped his head knowingly in a gesture that is universally understood to mean *non compos mentis*. Simultaneously he rattled off something in Chinese. The major frowned, nodded, and barked a command. The next thing the kid knew, he was stumbling along at bayonet point toward a temporary prisoners' stockade. A long, ramshackle building was situated in its center and two guard towers had been thrown up hastily, one at the entrance gate and the second behind the building. The gate opened and they gave the kid a push. He stumbled through and fell. It was still early morning. Off in the distance a cock crowed.

It shoulda been a bell, the kid thought, his mind floating free from the body he was sure was pouring its life substance from its enemy-inflicted wounds. *Instead of some damn rooster cock-a-doodle-dooing, the goddamned Reds oughta toll a bell.* The swirling blackness was closing in. The quality of hard contempt remained with him. *Well, come on, you Grim Reaper bastard, you got me. So finish the job. Quit stalling around.*

Hands lifted him and voices spoke softly. "Easy there. Easy. You're going to be all right."

What the hell? What was going on? (Was Death trying to play some grim joke on him?) His voice was thick, unintelligible.

"Watch it. That's it, Red. Now lay him here on this bench."

"Shall we strip his clothes off, Father?"

"Yes. And someone heat some hot water."

Red? Father? Hot water?

He fell deeper into the blackness, spinning around and

around. Again he tried to speak and couldn't. His thoughts wouldn't track. The voices were only blurs of meaningless sound. There seared through him, then, an exquisite, intolerable pain. It began in his left shoulder without forewarning. He jerked involuntarily and a scream tried to burst from his lips. The pain had revealed to him all the brilliant, blinding colors of the spectrum. The colors, for a time speck so volatile, froze. In another instant they were gone. Nothing remained.

The kid had fainted.

When he opened his eyes, someone was standing over him, changing a dressing on his shoulder wound. His tongue was dry and thick but he managed to get the words out: "I know this is probably a stupid question. But am I alive or dead?"

"What would be your guess?" a pleasant voice asked. It belonged to the man standing over him.

"Me, I'd buck the odds and say I'm still around."

"And I'd say you also very courageously bucked the odds when you volunteered for that diversionary mission which saved your company."

"How the hell do you know about that? Who are you?"

"A friend who has done his humble best with other friends here to help you."

"Why?"

Because this friend was a chaplain of the Catholic faith, also a prisoner, who had been captured a week earlier with Red and a dozen others. They were all that remained of a company attacked as the kid's had been and virtually wiped out. While the kid had been unconscious, he had relived the horrible experience he had been through. That was how they knew where he had come from and what he had done.

"Yeah," the kid said glumly, "and I left eighteen other guys out there dead." He wanted to argue with them about its being a "horrible experience," but he was still too weak and his head throbbed and pounded. Probably, too, he owed the padre and these other guys a word of thanks for saving his life. He knew for certain he did when he was told how, crudely but effectively, they had cauterized his wounds and improvised other surgical miracles without anesthetic (the cauterizing had knocked him cold), drugs, equipment, or, for that matter, experience.

"I guess I'm in hock to you people," he said.

"You might give thanks to God," the chaplain suggested.

The kid demurred. "I don't think God's interested in me,

and I know I'm not interested in Him. So don't try to get me on my knees, Padre."

A shout from the gate outside interrupted the discussion. More POWs, almost fifty of them this time, were being marched down the road to the stockade. Among them were wounded. The chaplain, Red, and the others did what they could for them. For a while the kid was forgotten. Late that night the chaplain dropped by to inquire how he felt.

"Okay," the kid said. The kid wanted to say more but he didn't quite know how to begin. He wanted to make the chaplain understand that the way he felt about God had nothing to do with him. God, then, to the kid, was simply another Authority figure.

The following day two more groups of POWs arrived and swelled the stockade's population to almost two hundred. Five had died before nightfall. Medical attention could have saved them all. Met with this complaint, the Reds looked at the dead impassively and said there would be a hospital and doctors where the POWs were going. "Nice conditions. Even pretty nurses. Everything."

At dawn the stockade was shouted awake and herded into trucks like cattle. A drive north to a permanent POW camp or city got underway over often almost impassable roads. On the second evening U.N. light bombers blew up a stretch of road and a motorized troop movement coming south. The Reds fumed and transferred their troops to the POW trucks. For the prisoners there began a long, grueling march north. The marchers were told repeatedly that they could thank the "American beasts" because they had to walk. The marchers grinned.

And many died. For you kept up or else. Brutally the weak and the infirm were separated from the strong and able-bodied. If you fell out, you were shot or bayoneted to death. You had to be able to take it to last. In spite of his painful, festering wounds, the kid lasted. And he taunted those who showed signs of weakening psychologically; he stung and drove many of the fainthearted with his jibes. The chaplain who had saved his life and he were like the good cop and the bad cop who pulled the old backroom trick to get what they wanted from a suspect; between them, between their encouragement and stinging abuse, they saved many lives. And a bond of sorts was formed, a grudging respect, an unqualified loyalty. They knew, when the men did not, they were working as a team, in just the sense that God and Satan are a team.

The marchers arrived at their destination at last, a huge prisoner city of almost three thousand men—and they learned fast what they were up against. The Reds expected "co-operation," an ugly word, as they defined it. Interrogation teams might go to work on you at any time and continue bombarding you with questions indefinitely until they got what they were after: some concrete evidence of a "reasonable attitude toward the peoples' cause." A propaganda broadcast, say, or a 'confession" of the belligerent intentions of the U.S. against Asia.

You would be exposed constantly to Communist political indoctrination. Attempts would be made to break your will to resist by starvation, fantastic lies, threats, "discipline" of a sort calculated to make your blood run cold at the thought of it. There would be rewards for your co-operation: a little more food, some medical attention, a tin of tobacco, enough clothing to keep you from freezing to death.

The progressives, the pros, they were called, the ones the Reds had wooed over, or the ones who considered it expedient always to align themselves with the top dog, had it easier. Mostly they were ignorant young men, ready dupes. A few, however, were animally cunning, with feral mentalities and the compulsive need to be boss. These were the dangerous ones. They betrayed and denounced and informed, making the miserable lot of their fellows far more difficult, occasionally altogether untenable.

The kid's actions on the march north had given his North Korean and Chinese captors an idea he could be induced to collaborate with them. But, from the time of his arrival at the sprawling POW camp, he jeered at their efforts both in private, at a rigged interrogation session, and before other POWs, at compulsory classes in communism. One Red "instructor" became so infuriated by his loss of face that he whipped the kid's chest, back, and legs with an Asian equivalent of a cat-o'-nine-tails until the kid's whole body was a bloody, lacerated mass of flesh.

The kid survived. He survived the best or the worst the enemy had to offer. Among his captors he became an awesome legend, an insane, grinning devil. Once they put the screws to him and he agreed to confess. He confessed that he had been snatched from a mental institution for violent patients. "Hell," he said, "that's where the U.S. Army got most of us. I thought you people knew that. We either came from nut houses or joints where they got the worst hoodlums locked up. You don't think they'd send anybody over here they gave a damn about, do you?" For some time this prize confession created a considerable stir among the Red big domes. He was full of stunts like that until starvation and mistreatment beat him down almost to the point of death. Still he grinned and hate sustained him.

The gentle and courageous young chaplain who had ministered to the kid following his capture and who had been a special target for persecution by the enemy was attacked by a raging fever and dysentery. A living skeleton now, it was obvious he wouldn't live long unless he received prompt medical attention. Notified of his condition, the guards either pretended not to understand or shrugged indifferently. The kid called on the last of his strength to raise hell and to get the others to do the same until he was allowed to talk with the camp's military commander and its chief political officer, both of whom spoke English. (This was at a time when peace talks had been renewed and the Reds were all seeming benevolence. On some levels, that is.)

"The padre needs a doctor bad," the kid said. "I think he's dying."

"No doctor," the political officer said.

The kid grinned and murder glittered in his sunken eyes. "You want him to die, don't you, you bowlegged little bastard?"

The slap cracked like a snapped tree branch.

"Pig! American slime! I should have you shot for insolence! The political officer's pitted face was mottled with rage. He barked some words of command in Chinese to one of the guards. This scowling fellow stepped forward, his submachine gun ready.

"Go ahead," the kid taunted, still grinning. "Tell your pinheaded stooge to shoot. And then tell the world what supermen you are. Uncle Mao'll probably give you a medal. *But get the padre a doctor!*"

The political officer, recalling with a shudder how earlier encounters with this fearless, imbecilic one had ended so disastrously, shook his head helplessly. "You handle this insane American dog," he snapped, and stalked off, vowing doubtless to take care of the kid when the present soft policy was canceled.

"Well?" the kid said.

88

The commandant was tough but not cruel. His look was speculative and a quirk of a smile appeared fleetingly at the corner of his lips. "I wasn't aware you were a religious man," he said.

"I'm not. What the hell's that got to do with it?"

"Nothing. I'll send a doctor."

"Thanks."

The commandant kept his word. Two hours later a Chinese doctor came to see the delirious chaplain.

"Hopeless case," the doctor said in pidgin English. "Die soon. Too bad." He left.

The kid cursed—and kept a long vigil. Some time after dawn the delirium slowly lifted and the chaplain's fever-bright eyes, set in a gaunt face, began to focus.

"It's me," the kid said. "How do you feel?"

"All right."

"Then that damn slant-eyed sawbones was wrong. You're going to be okay."

The chaplain knew the Chinese doctor hadn't been wrong. He didn't doubt that he was dying. But this was no cause for alarm. He waited for the end calmly, without fear. He prayed and then he spoke in a whisper to the kid about an unwrathful God, an unviolent future, a better world. His last words to the kid were "Seek Him, put hate behind you, and try to find yourself."

The kid looked long at the chaplain's wasted body with its bloated abdomen. *The padre was a good guy,* the kid thought. *He had guts.*

And faith.

And he was dead. The kid wasn't.

Chapter Thirteen

THE SHOOTING BATTLE ENDED—later. And following a great deal of high-and medium-level wrangling Korea was divided at a conference table.

Emaciated from his months of captivity and deloused, the kid was among the third group of POWs to be exchanged. He resembled more nearly a fumigated skeleton with parchment-like skin stretched across its bones than he did a living human being. When the photographers from the news services asked him to pose for pictures, he invited them politely to go to hell.

"You're a hero, soldier," one of them said good-naturedly. "A returning hero. So give us a big smile."

"You dumb bastards," the kid said without malice. "Don't you know that the heroes are all dead?"

Hospitalized for a few weeks in Japan, fed thick steaks and pumped full of vitamins, he lost that fugitive-from-a-boneyard look. Dentists had him "open wide," peered, poked, and drilled. Then came the sessions with the boys from Army Intelligence, the sharpies with more questions than a TV quizmaster. Had he been mistreated, or had he seen anyone mistreated, by the enemy? Where? When? How?

To these questions, the kid had a stock reply. "If they gave me a bad time," he said, "maybe I asked for it. I got no beef."

"But can't you see?" he was told. "It's important that we know."

The kid couldn't see that. He personally wasn't convinced it was important—or, for that matter, that it made the least damned bit of difference—that his interrogators know what had happened to him as a POW. Besides, his peculiar code wouldn't let him complain of the brutal treatment accorded him by his captors.

"I'm ready to forget it," he replied. And if they pushed him, gently of course, he would say, "I don't remember,"

90

and his flashing eyes would dare them to call him a liar.

Well, then, they would say, trying another tack, what information could he supply on that lanky sergeant with the southern drawl who had chosen to remain behind? Or on the young corporal in his outfit who had informed on his fellow POWs? Or on that looie from the West Coast who had confessed that the United States was waging germ warfare? Or—on the brainwashed, the weak, the toadies, the fools, the cowards, the confused?

"What can I tell you about those guys? Nothing. You signed me up to fight, not fink."

"Yes, of course. We sympathize with your feelings. Yet we want to see justice done."

"Justice? What the hell is justice? I'll tell you. It's just a word that means anything you say it does."

"You have a duty to tell us, a duty both as a soldier and a citizen."

"That's a laugh. And if I don't tell you, assuming I know something, then I suppose you'll toss me into the army pen at Fort Leavenworth. I'll probably get twenty years for not turning stool pigeon."

"You realize, of course, that you're making it most difficult for us."

"Unh-unh. You're making it difficult for yourselves."

That ended the interrogation. "Unco-operative and uncommunicative," his file read. That same file also contained accounts by field officers of the kid's insatiable hunger for battle, his suicidal fearlessness. Copies of statements by other POWs began to fill that file too, telling how the kid had risked his hide to steal food for this GI or help that one escape; how, too, he had boldly stood up to the enemy and the pros alike, grinning and telling them to drop dead, and how that enemy had subjected him as a result to corrective discipline, so called, that would have destroyed first the mind and then the body of another man.

After carefully reviewing the file, one doctor shook his head sadly. "An unusual and tragic case," he commented aloud.

A colleague agreed. It obviously couldn't be handled routinely. "Then you believe, as Dr. Byrde and I do, that intensive psychotherapy is needed?"

"I do."

The kid was flown to a VA hospital in the States. There, impatient for a discharge, he spent several more weeks. On arrival he demanded suspiciously, "How come I got sent to this loony bin?" He'd seen the heavy screens on the windows.

"The doctors in Japan recommended a thorough checkup."

"What kind of a checkup?"

"Dr. Merson will explain everything when she has a talk with you tomorrow."

That afternoon at a staff meeting the kid's case was discussed at length. Dr. Edith Merson, a tiny and spectacled person with a motherly appearance and a well-earned reputation as one of the country's top psychiatrists, was one of those participating.

The kid spent a restless night. In the morning his door opened and a smiling, gray-haired woman entered. "Good morning," she said. "I'm Dr. Merson."

"You're the one that's supposed to tell me what I'm doing in this nut factory?"

The gray head nodded briskly. "I am." She adjusted her head mirror and began an examination of the kid's eyes. "The doctors who saw you in Japan thought we might be able to help you."

"I can look out for myself okay. I don't need any help from headshrinkers."

The pupils were round and equal and reacted promptly to light and convergence; cornea and sclerae were clear; conjunctivae were not injected; the extraocular muscles were intact; visual fields were normal to confrontation test.

"In that case," said Dr. Merson. "I'm sure you won't mind giving us some help."

"How?"

"By answering some questions."

"What kind of questions?"

"About yourself and your experiences."

"Why do you want to know?"

"It would help us understand men like yourself."

The kid thought this over. He didn't like the idea of their using a woman psychiatrist. It put him on the defensive. A man he could have told to go to hell.

The ophthalmoscope revealed no edema of the optic nerve head. Well, there had been no reason to suspect organic brain damage. Still, one always had to eliminate all possibilities and not resort to hunches or guesswork. This afternoon the young man was scheduled to have an electroencephalogram. (The tracings would be within normal limits. There

92

would be some interesting variations, but their clinical significance would be doubtful.)

"Look," the kid said, "all I want is a piece of paper that
says I'm discharged. So do me a favor and find another
guinea pig."

"The months you spent at the prisoner-of-war camp must
have been a grueling ordeal."

"I'm not complaining."

"Then, having passed the tests imposed by a ruthless
enemy under the most brutal conditions, I can't see why you
should be afraid to take ours."

"Ma'am, don't talk like that. I didn't say anything about
being afraid. You're trying to drive me into a corner with
words."

Dr. Merson handed the kid a pencil and a blank piece of
white, tablet-size paper. "Draw a picture of a man and a
woman for me, if you will, please."

"Is this a gag or a trick?"

"Neither, I assure you."

"Which one do you want me to draw first?"

"That's up to you."

The kid drew the man first, on the right half of the paper.
He was a hard-faced young adult, with a muscular, broad-
shouldered body that was disproportionate to his smaller
head. The woman was perfectly proportioned and fully
clothed. She was an older woman. A quality of gentleness
showed itself in her face. The man towered over her, like an
evil force. They weren't looking at one another.

"Let me see what you've drawn." Dr. Merson took the
paper and examined it. "The woman is your mother," she
suggested, not making the words a question.

"My mother's dead. She's been dead a long time."

"And your father, is he dead, too?"

"You got the records. It's all there. And if it's all the
same to you I'd just as soon not talk about my old man or
my mother or anything like that."

"Very well. Now, I'm going to speak some words aloud
and as I do I want you to tell me what word comes to your
mind. For example, when I say 'love' what word do you
think of?"

The kid was about to say "hate" when he checked himself.
This could be a trap. He had to watch himself. "Maybe I don't
think of any word," he said.

"Everyone does," Dr. Merson assured him.

93

They went through a long list of words three times—and a clear pattern had begun to form by the time they had finished.

Negative words with a special meaning to the kid he did not associate with one of their antonyms, for they were more than a casual part of his vocabulary. They were a dynamic part of his life. Mention one—"hate," say, or "guile" or "violence"—and they all came flooding into his consciousness. With affirmative words such as "love," on the other hand, there simply was a rejection that never reached a conscious level. *For example, . . . love . . .* That was how the doctor had begun this deadly associative game. Well, love was dead. But that was only part of it. Hate wasn't. Nor a need.

(The violence behind him—the warping childhood violence, the hardening reformatory violence, the suicidally intoxicating battle violence, and the deadening POW camp violence—these had created and left in their wake a demanding emotional hunger that gnawed like a huge and hungry rat at his entrails.

(Ironically, he wasn't dead; he should have been and even in a way he was, for when, in battle, he had killed, coldly and joyously killed again and again, he had killed something in himself. But it wasn't the sickness in his soul he had killed; it was the hope he ever would be free again, or whole or normal.

(And the ashes of this hope were entombed in a death wish, while above them were the last words of a dead priest: *Seek Him, put hate behind you, and try to find yourself.* But how could you see the sky and know its glory when your eyes were sightless and you were chained in a windowless dungeon? How could you expect mind doctors to help you when all the evidence pointed to the fact that you were beyond help? You didn't dare break your rule to mistrust every living person. You had to find your own way.)

The kid spent all of the following morning hours in the office of one of the hospital's psychologists, a tall, stooped man, middle-aged, with a long face and a booming voice.

"First on the agenda are some photographs of people's faces," the psychologist explained. "Take a good look at them and then pick out the two you like the most and, after that, the two you dislike the most."

The kid studied the eight faces laid out on the table in

94

front of him. "Hell," he said, "they all look like a bunch of nuts to me."

The psychologist made no effort to repress a smile. "They may be. But," he continued amiably, "is that any reason why you shouldn't like some and dislike others?"

"I guess not," the kid said. His eyes returned to the pictures. "Let's see. This one and . . . yeah, and this one."

"Fine. Now the two you don't like."

"Well, I don't think much of this weird-looking old gink here or this crazy-eyed dame here."

The psychologist nodded. They continued through the series. (The test would be repeated each morning for a week.) Next came the ink blots.

"It looks like two witches fighting over a broom," he said initially of one card.

"Do they look human?"

"No."

Action he saw aplenty; but the figures on the cards never were quite human. (And this was true, too, of the people he met, himself included.) He reacted especially to the red-stained cards and the black ones.

"This one looks like— *What the hell!*

"Yes?" the psychologist prompted.

"What kind of smart goddamned deal is this?"

"What do you mean?"

The kid was about to blurt out that it looked like a woman's external sexual organs when he shut the words off. These smart bastards maybe were trying to trip him up and make him out some kind of sex freak. That would give them a good excuse to keep him locked up. "It reminds me of a map," he said.

"Anything else?"

"A crab."

"And . . . ?"

"Nothing." He'd thrown up his defenses.

Calmly the psychologist said, "Most people see a woman's private parts. At first I thought you had, too."

"Oh," the kid said sarcastically, inviting the other's wrath, "they pay you to think, too, do they? I thought all you had to do was play stupid games with these goddamned ink blot things and ask a lot of silly questions."

"I'm sorry if I made you angry," the psychologist said. "I didn't mean to."

There were more tests involving the projective technique,

95

and intelligence and educational achievement level tests as well. For the kid it was like being held in a doorless room whose walls kept slowly closing in. If he had refused defiantly to take the tests, they had him. They had him equally when he took them, when he tried to grin and out-guess them. This way he was playing their game and only a sucker did that. But, having co-operated, having given them a look inside himself, couldn't he still make them play his game in the end? He thought he could. And he bided his time.

One day Dr. Merson brought along another psychiatrist, a Dr. Rader, to see him. Dr. Rader was short, balding, on the plump side, with dark eyes that bored hypnotically into you and never seemed to blink; and his Viennese accent was so thick you had to listen carefully to understand him. Dr. Merson did most of the talking but every four or five minutes Dr. Rader would interrupt to fire a seemingly irrelevant question at the kid. What was the kid's favorite color? Had he ever thought he was dying? Had he been a bed-wetter? Did he smoke?

The kid, pretending not to understand, made the doctor repeat each question three or four times. He gave answers that didn't satisfy the little man at all and eased himself into the plump doctor's face. "Now it's my turn to ask the jackpot question. When do we stop picking at my brains like a bunch of vultures and give me a discharge?"

It was the doctor then who failed to understand.

"I thought so," the kid said.

"You'll be interviewed at conference as soon as all the necessary material dealing with your situation has been complied and evaluated," Dr. Merson said soothingly.

Dr. Rader nodded verification and smiled encouragement. The kid grinned. "I'll be waiting."

He sat facing them, five doctors seated in a row behind a long table. All five wore cheerful countenances, including Drs. Merson and Rader.

"How do you feel?"

He didn't say "Okay," and wait like a good little boy for the next question. Instead, he seized the initiative, determined to force a showdown. He'd planned his strategy in advance. This time he had to fight with words rather than fists. And he had to win.

"I got something to say and all I ask is that you hear me out before you people go into your song and dance. I been

96

thinking and I decided that you're not any better than the Reds. They tried to make me think one way and you're trying to make me think another, and because I don't and won't you want to lock me up."

He saw their startled looks and plunged forward remorselessly. "I was good enough to go to Korea and fight like hell and get my ass shot off and wind up doing a lot of months in a POW camp. But now I ain't good enough to get turned loose. I ain't good enough to be a civilian. That's a laugh." He laughed.

His sudden attack had knocked them off balance and he intended to keep them that way. "So maybe I don't like cops and people like that who give orders and got weight to throw around." Maybe he didn't like authority. That didn't mean he was a ding, did it? Who the hell did they think they were trying to kid, asking him a lot of damnfool questions and giving him all those absurd tests and putting on a big show, as though they knew what they were doing!

Maybe the Reds had been right.

He continued to slash away. Sure he was being unfair. He was putting them in an impossible position deliberately. It was the only way. They were right about him but he knew they couldn't prove it, not the way you prove a man guilty in court. He told them how it was: they'd either give him a discharge with no strings or he'd get himself a lawyer and take his case to the newspapers. He'd put his war record up against their ink blots.

"Which is it going to be?"

Very politely they thanked him, they didn't say for what, and then they excused him. Their smiles had frozen on their faces and he believed he had won. It didn't matter that he had done so by dirty tactics. He knew he had won for sure the next day when he had an unexpected visitor, his sister Janey.

"Surprised to see me, Buddy?"

"Hell, yes." He was surprised all right—and suspicious.

She was well. She said "they" had helped her get well. Then he got the point and purpose of the visit: "they" could help him, too. All he had to do was sign a paper voluntarily asking for a commitment to VA custody. She promised to stand by him.

He talked to her tough. "I don't know what kind of crap they fed you but there's nothing wrong with me. Nothing!" Then he asked her about herself and learned how, finally,

97

she had won her long fight against tuberculosis. "Well," he said, "this is one fight I got to win, too. In my own way."

His medical folder was marked: "Diagnosis: psychopathic personality, without psychosis. Prognosis: poor." They knew he was headed for serious trouble but were powerless to intervene.

His discharge came through. He then was on his own, a civilian again, with a pocketful of back pay and even some medals. He visited Janey once and then he disappeared for a while.

Chapter Fourteen

THEREAFTER, the kid would always remember that morning. It was the morning Maura came into his life. He got up about eight, after the sun had poured in through the east window of his room, so golden and thick it seemed almost liquid. He stood there in the raw, stretching, feeling good in spite of himself. From three stories below the sounds of the city, now harmonious and blending, now discordant and full of strident contention, reached him, and he grinned. The city was like himself—a changing thing, its ways and purposes not always predictable.

He took his time under the needle-point shower, letting the hot, then cold streams of water sting his scarred, unbecoming pelt. He had no place to go, really nothing to do except maybe take in a show or something like that to kill time. Yet within him was a growing sense of expectancy, which didn't make any sense at all.

Hell, he thought, *outside of Janey there's nobody that knows and gives a damn whether I even exist or not.* More than ever he felt the aloneness crowding in on him and now it was turning into loneliness. Briefly, then, the good feeling —the suspect and alien good feeling—became a grain-of-sand-at-the ocean feeling. He was lost again. And angry.

His mind was like a piece of ground glass through which reality was filtered, and in the process magnified and distorted; and from reality his mind drew not only light, illumination, but an inflammable heat. Often, too often, it burned painfully and started a fire in his emotions.

He felt better when, briskly toweling his lean wet body, he cursed his questing, emotional pyromaniac mind. By the time he had dressed, he was able to laugh. At first it was a mirthless, sardonic laugh. But then he recalled how, a couple of days earlier, a glib-tongued salesman at a clothing store had tried to sell him a *pink* shirt! Oh, brother! He laughed a fat man's belly-jiggling, thigh-slapping laugh—and his thoughts started to free-wheel.

99

Pink shirts he associated with that VA headshrinker who had asked him those loaded questions about colors, especially the one about what his favorite color was. Well, the answer was still the same: sometimes it was black, which he'd read somewhere wasn't really a color at all, and sometimes it was red. (Sometimes it was death; sometimes it was violence.) Lately it was mostly black. Not an ordinary black, though. A black with a brilliance, an intensity that would either dazzle and blind any chance psychological Peeping Tom or that would camouflage completely the purpose it hid.

He took a long walk, letting his long, leanly muscled legs carry him where they would, while simultaneously he engaged in a mental excursion that really took him nowhere. He walked and thought about everything and nothing for perhaps an hour, until his stomach set up a clamor for food. It was hunger, then—and chance?—that led him to the restaurant, a middle-class eating place at the edge of the financial district. He entered, standing momentarily near the door while his eyes accommodated themselves to the subdued interior, when he saw there were only tables, no counter. He was about to turn and walk out, thinking the eatery wasn't his speed, when he saw her.

He sensed in that first instant that the good feeling had been premonitory. It should have put him on guard. He'd had it before in Korea, when some sixth sense told him enemy troops were around, although there had been no sign of them. He'd felt alive at those times, intensely so, and yet he had never been closer to death. Now death could not be near—he'd outrun death for a while—but here was some new danger. *She* was a danger

With an effort he stopped staring at her and turned toward the nearest table. Reaching it, he slid the chair back and seated himself. He picked up and pretended to study the menu as she came across the room. He felt the excitement rise in him.

"Good morning, sir," she said. Her voice was Eve's but it also could have been Lilith's. It was soft, like a shy caress, and yet not suggestive.

He looked up to see her standing there with a pencil poised over her order pad. She had scrubbed, wholesome look. Her hair, done in a bun at the back, was the color of ripe wheat. Her violet-colored eyes were slightly, very slightly, almond-shaped. She used no make-up but a touch of lipstick. Her starched waitress's uniform did not conceal, nor did it advertise, a deep and generous bosom. She wasn't tall. She smiled easily, naturally. About her was nothing artificial, no big-city sophistication.

"Is it too late to get some breakfast?" the kid asked.

"No, sir," she said. "What would you like, sir?"

"First, if it's all the same with you, I'd like for you to skip the 'sir.' Then I'd like a couple of waffles and an order of ham and eggs."

"Yes, sir," she said, and then their eyes met and they laughed together. "I mean, yes," she corrected, taking down the order. "What would you like to drink? Some orange joice? Coffee?"

"Milk," the kid said.

It was a good breakfast, prepared the way he liked it; yet when she brought it, smiling, he found that he was no longer hungry. Rather, he was no longer belly-hungry. He ate mechanically, unable to concentrate on the food, and once he almost knocked his glass of milk to the floor. All the while his eyes hungrily followed her as she waited on two fussy, middle-aged ladies and then on a jolly fat man with three chins and two briefcases. If she was aware of his scrutiny, she gave no sign. No girl—no woman—had ever affected him in this way before. And yet there was something about her that was familiar. She reminded him in a way he couldn't put his finger on of someone he had known well. This puzzled him. For certainly this oddly pretty girl resembled physically no one in his past. She was unique in that respect.

The kid left an egg, one of the waffles, and two strips of bacon untouched. She noticed this when she answered his signal that he was ready to leave. Her smile was tentative and there was a note of worry in her voice when she asked, "Is something wrong, sir?" She had forgotten again about the "sir," and had added it out of force of habit, or she had rejected his request, electing to keep their casual customer-waitress relationship on an impersonal level, especially since he had been gawking at her so. He wasn't certain which was the case.

"Is something wrong?" he repeated. "Not with the service or the food," he added quickly, bitterly aware of his marked limitations with words. When he had to he could convey ironies—but not subtleties. For him the English language was either a bludgeoning weapon or a strictly utilitarian tool, and a clumsy one. He could use it to taunt but not to tease, to wound but not to heal wounds, to destroy rapport but not under difficult circumstances to establish it. There were times, and this was one of those times, when his vocabulary was unequal to the urgent imagery of his mind. He was good at visualizing but not verbalizing. And because all this was so, he blotted out the delicate imagery with crude anger.

"Here," he said, scowling. He'd shoved a five-dollar bill at her. Dumbly, she took the money. He saw the hurt in her eyes before he walked away. Typically, he'd groped his way toward her only to make her recoil. Now he could try to convince himself that he had been the one to do the rejecting.

She called out, "Just a moment, sir, and I'll get you your change."

He spun around and paused only long enough to tell her savagely, "Goddamn my change!"

On reaching the sidewalk, he squinted against the brilliance and the glare of the day. He had forgotten about the sun. All his life, in moments of stress, he had been doing that. It was time to change. There were mnemonic disciplines for the senses as well as for the mind. For thawing emotions, too. There had to be. The VA squirrel doctors had thought he was some kind of nut, hadn't they? Well, he was ready to admit—to himself, not to them—that they were right. But that didn't mean he was ready to admit he couldn't personally do something about it. He could and he would. What he needed, he told himself, wasn't some big-domed psychiatric mechanic to make any fancy adjustments on his "personality structure," whatever the hell that was.

What I need is her! Awareness hit him with the force of a physical blow. But how could he know that? How could he be sure? He brushed the questions aside with others: Who said he had to be sure? Who said he had to stop and nicely analyze? All right, so he'd only seen her once. Was the validity of the way he felt to be determined by a stop watch or some long-winded psychological theory. As far as he was concerned, chronology and hypothesis were unwelcomed interlopers. He wanted no part of them.

He learned her name by phoning the restaurant from down the street and asking. "Maura." He said the name to himself over and over. *Maura. Maura.* He found that he was whistling a hit song he had heard blaring from the jukeboxes. It was a ballad that stressed affirmatively, if somewhat vapidly, the marvelous and magic virtues of romantic love. When he became conscious of what he was doing, he frowned.

Love.

102

What did he know about love? Nothing. Nothing at all. And yet, he believed, too much. Or too many of the wrong things? Which? The damned questions again. More of them than answers. Well, he'd keep it simple. It would get complicated soon enough, without any help from him.

Love was a word. And Maura was a girl.

He was at the restaurant again the following morning and the morning after that. But she wasn't there. A tall, thin girl wearing glasses was working in her place. With an elaborate show of unconcern he asked about her. These were her days off, he learned. He didn't see her until the morning of the third day. He felt as though at least an eternity had passed.

When she set eyes on him, she looked startled. She hesitated several seconds before she came over to take his order. Her oval face was grave.

"I'm sorry I acted like I did when I was here before," he said.

"It's all right," she told him slowly.

"Can I call you by your first name?" he asked. "They told me what it was."

"If you want to."

He did, very much. "Thanks," he said. "Thanks . . . Maura."

Every day after that for the rest of the month the kid ate his breakfast and lunch at the restaurant. He and Maura would exchange a few words about the weather or some equally impersonal topic and they would share a smile. During the meal his eyes would follow her and once, shyly but not coyly, she asked him why he watched her so much.

He could have said, "It's because . . . well, it's kind of hard to explain, but I guess you could say it's just because I like to watch you. Seeing you laugh and smile and everything makes me feel good in a funny way." But the question was, Why? Why did she fascinate him? Why this particular girl?

"It's because you remind me of my mother," he heard himself reply aloud, aware then that his mind had answered the questions that long had troubled him, too. For his reply had been perfectly truthful, even though he did not fully understand its implications himself. Maura did in fact remind him of his mother. And she did because he had loved his mother and now, he realized, he loved Maura. (He had loved his mother when he was fearful and weak, and because of his fear and his weakness his love had failed her. He had failed her. Failure and guilt had made him what he was. They had driven him to strike a bargain with hate and guile. Now he wanted, in a sense, another mother. Without

103

being aware of it, that was what he had been seeking all along.)

He wanted Maura. He wanted to love her, cherish her, protect her from a world he knew to be menacing and hostile. He needed her more than he needed life. (He needed her to act out his neurotic anxiety, to project his hate usefully, to prove his strength and his manhood. And unless the twin needs for air to breathe and food to eat are selfish or unselfish, his need for Maura was neither one nor the other. It simply was.)

Shortly after Maura had her hours changed, from eight to four to four to twelve, and the kid began dropping in for a late meal, Maura consented to let him walk her home. The third night she invited him in. Her second-floor rear apartment was tiny and spotless. On a table was a picture of an elderly couple and nine children, one of whom was unmistakably Maura.

"This is my family," Maura said. At the kid's request, after making some hot chocolate for them both, she told him about herself. She had been born and raised on a farm in the Midwest. She had two older brothers; six brothers and sisters, three of each, had been born after her. The family had not always had it easy financially but they had managed.

Maura's girlhood had been unremarkable. (When she met the kid she was only nineteen.) The year before, following her graduation from a rural high school, she had been introduced to a handsome character in his early thirties who, at the time, had been involved in some sort of grandiose scheme to promote uranium stock. When he had gone off to close what he had told her would be a tremendous deal that would put him on easy street for life, the family had been relieved. They hadn't liked him.

"But I did," Maura said. "I thought I was in love with him. And when he wrote me I was so happy I could sing. He told me he loved me and needed me. He begged me to come to the city, and from the way his letter was worded I thought he wanted to marry me. My father forbade me to go but I ran off. I thought I had a right to live my own life."

"Did you marry this guy?" the kid asked.

"No," Maura said. "When I met him he was broke. He told me his business partners had double-crossed him but later I found out that the government had got after him. I told him that his not having any money didn't make any difference, not

104

if he loved me. I said I was willing to marry him right away, regardless."

"What happened?"

The big dealer confessed to Maura that he was already married. But, he said, the marriage had been a mistake. He pictured his wife as a cold, grasping woman. She, he continued, had refused him a divorce until and unless he gave her a large cash settlement. That, he claimed, was why he had needed and wanted the money so badly. Deeply moved, Maura proved nevertheless that she was not altogether naïve, nor a too-willing tool.

"He wanted to use me," Maura said. "In fact, he tried to."

He ruthlessly involved her as an innocent front in one of his shady, high-pressure promotional deals, this time in oil. When she discovered its true—and fraudulent—nature, she strongly objected. Smoothness and charm didn't work, so he got ugly. He told her she would wind up behind bars too if she didn't co-operate and do exactly what he told her. Nobody, he claimed, would believe she had been only a stupid, country girl dupe. And when she still balked he crudely threatened to write her parents an anonymous letter telling them she was "shacked up and operating with a con man," which was a blatant lie. "The odd part," Maura said, "is that he never once tried to get fresh with me, not even when he was doing all these other things."

On this latter score the kid felt relief, but at the same time he felt hot anger knot and writhe in his belly. "What did you do?" he asked harshly.

"I pretended to give in to him," Maura answered. "But that night I packed my bag and ran off. I didn't know what else to do. I was scared and all mixed up."

Maura had only a few odd dollars in her purse. She spent them on a bus ticket. The bus took her through the night to another city. She arrived in the early morning, broke and hungry. Convinced that she had disgraced her parents and that she might even be wanted by the police, she was afraid to turn to either her mother and father or the cops. She walked aimlessly for hours. At one point she felt so desperate, so depressed, so *alone* she even considered flinging herself from a bridge she crossed. Then she came to a church.

"I went in and prayed," Maura said. "And God must have heard me." For when she opened her eyes she found the elderly pastor of the church at her side. "He took me to the little parsonage beside the church and had his wife fix me a meal. They were both very kind."

Maura stayed with them that night. The next day the pastor helped her find this tiny apartment, paid the landlady two weeks' rent in advance, and gave her enough pocket money to tide her over until she could find work. Through the employment office, she had secured her present job as a waitress at the restaurant.

"That was about six months ago," Maura said, "and here I am. I guess it's not a very exciting life but I like it. I've saved a little money and of course I repaid the pastor. I go to his church every Sunday and to prayer meeting Wednesday nights."

"Don't you have any boy friends?" the kid asked.

Maura blushed. "No," she said, conceding shyly that perhaps her painful experience with the smoothie who had tried to exploit her had made her afraid, in a way, of men.

"Are you afraid of me?"

Maura shook her head at the kid's blunt question. She said she wasn't. Why not? "Well, because you usually look so sad and lonely, even when you're smiling. Are you? I mean, has something happened to you, too?"

"A lot of things have happened to me," the kid said. "But one look at my beat-up face probably told you that."

"I think it's a good face," Maura said.

"Just because it's grinning most of the time, don't let it fool you. It's only a mask."

"What's behind the mask?"

"A guy," the kid said; "a crazy stranger."

"Would you like to let me meet him?"

"It wouldn't be a good idea. Not yet at least."

"You said I reminded you of your mother. Does she live with you?"

"She's dead." The kid forced himself to add, "She committed suicide."

"Oh!" Maura cried, stricken. "I'm sorry. I didn't—"

"It's all right," the kid said. "It's getting late, though, so I think I'd better shove off."

"Will I see you again?"

"Do you want to?"

"Yes," Maura said. "I do. And please forgive me . . . "

"Forget it. Just forget it."

"I can't."

Neither could the kid. And he had Maura inside him. She

106

was there with the sickness. *Run!* he told himself. *Run for her sake. You found her too late.* But the dead chaplain's words held him, mocked him, haunted him. He didn't run. He couldn't. He stayed away from the restaurant for several days, walking the streets as Maura had, fighting a battle with himself.

If you just need a woman, buy one. Go to a cat house. He did. But it was no good. The whore led him to a not large, sparsely furnished bedroom, the "trick room," he knew it was called. Inside he paid her the amount specified: twenty dollars. The whore disrobed then, unself-consciously. With a face and body that were almost bovine, she stood before him naked. Instead of chewing her cud, she was chewing gum, making it pop.

"I've changed my mind," the kid said. "Keep the twenty for your troubles."

The whore shrugged indifferently. The kid got out of there, fast, fighting down the temptation to run—or vomit. He walked for miles and he came close to breaking his vow never to drink.

Finally he decided: *I'll see Maura one more time. I'll tell her the truth. Then I'll leave for good. Then she'll be glad to have me go. She'll know what a no-good sonofabitch I am.*

He went to her apartment early in the evening of one of her days off. When she answered his knock, he saw that her eyes were red-rimmed. She obviously had been crying.

"I didn't think you would be back," Maura said quietly, smiling. "I was afraid . . . "

"I got something to tell you," the kid said, his voice hard. He entered and she closed the door behind him.

"Yes?"

He took a breath and began. "I just got out of the Army. They almost didn't let me out because they thought I was a nut. They were probably right. I must be. I killed a lot of guys on the other side, little rice-eating, bandy-legged jokers I'd never seen in a place I'd never heard of, and I liked it. You hear that? Goddammit, I liked killing 'em! That's why I joined up in the first place, not because I was patriotic or anything like that."

He gulped more air into his lungs and went on. "Well, I got shot up and caught and I did a lot of time in a POW camp. I lived like an animal, I was treated like one, and I think I turned into one. Or maybe, probably, I was one long before that. I've been in trouble ever since I was a little kid.

When I was in my teens I did two stretches in a reform school and before that I was in an orphanage. I told you my mother committed suicide but I didn't tell you why or where. She did it in prison and she'd gone to prison for shooting my old man dead. He was no damned good and I turned out just like him. So now you know about me. I wanted you to before I left for good because otherwise you just might be sorry I was gone."

Maura took the kid's knuckle-smashed right hand in her own small one. "I don't want you to go, soldier. I want you to stay." Then she looked up at him, meeting his turbulent eyes. "You see," she said simply, "I love you."

"You can't," the kid said. "You can't love the guy I just told you about."

"That's right, soldier, I can't. The man I love is the one you're trying to keep hidden from me. Please," Maura said. "Please, soldier. Tell me about him."

She knows! the kid thought. He cursed silently. He was shaking.

She waited.

"There was a chaplain in the POW camp with me," the kid finally said. He told Maura then about the chaplain, their shared experiences, and the chaplain's dying words. He told her, too, about his sister Janey, whose tuberculosis finally had been arrested. He told her last the most difficult thing to tell of all: that he was afraid of himself and the sickness inside himself, afraid that Maura would be hurt if he didn't leave.

"Soldier, my soldier!" Maura cried. "I know you'd never hurt me. And we can be happy together. We can have the life we've always wanted. It will be a good life, soldier, a wonderful life, if you will only give love a chance."

Give love a chance! Maura's quiet, intense words were written in fire in the kid's mind. His need of Maura was acute. But did he have the right to expose her to the danger that hate cunningly might contrive to betray them? He wavered. Love was the only thing in this life that he feared and the one thing that could make him whole and free.

The kid raised his left hand and let it rest gently on the girl's shoulder. "Can I kiss you, Maura?"

"Yes," Maura whispered.

Later the kid said, "I love you, Maura."

"I'm glad, soldier."

"I hope it works out for us."

"It will!" Maura said fiercely. "I know it will!"

108

Chapter Fifteen

"WE'RE MARRIED, soldier!" Maura said delightedly. "We're man and wife!" She was enchanted.

It was true. It wasn't a dream. The elderly pastor had married them that afternoon.

Standing stiffly erect in his new business suit, white shirt, and plain blue tie, the kid had heard Maura say a soft yet emphatic "I do" to the pastor's traditional question. He had listened as the question had been repeated, with his name substituted.

Did he, the kid, take this oddly pretty girl in the simple white bridal gown, standing proudly beside him, to be his lawfully wedded wife?

He did. God, yes, he did.

Then they had been pronounced man and wife. They had been made one; "bone of my bones, and flesh of my flesh," as it said in Genesis. Yet in the ceremonial words themselves, in the due registration of the fact of the nuptials, and in the wedding band he had placed on her finger, there was no uniting magic. There was, rather, such magic only in the power of their love and its ability to withstand the trials it would face and every attack made upon it. Its greatest enemy would be hate, and hate too would be its severest prosecutor and judge.

Below them the sea glistened, the waves silver-tipped in the moonlight. They stood looking down, not speaking at first, content to feel the night around them. Off in the distance a night bird sang hauntingly.

The kid was calm now. As one erases chalk from a blackboard, he wiped the streaks of doubt momentarily from his mind. The inner turbulence, the violence of spirit drifted slowly away with a softly whispering breeze.

The world was theirs, his and Maura's, and they had it to themselves. They had selected this cottage above the ocean as the place to spend their honeymoon. The dull throbbing

109

boom of the surf told him the choice had been a perfect one. And to think that those VA psychiatrists had wanted him to agree to stay locked up! He shuddered when he realized that if he had, he never would have met this young wife whose hand he held.

"Cold, soldier?" Maura asked.

The kid shook his head. "No, but I'm getting a little hungry."

Maura smiled. "I'm not surprised. Neither one of us has had a bite to eat since breakfast. So, my lord and master," she said laughingly, "if you'll just step inside, your humble wife will be happy to prepare your dinner."

The kid frowned. "Maura, please don't call me anything like that again, huh? I mean . . . well, I just don't like the sound of words like 'lord and master,' not even when they're used jokingly."

"All right, soldier."

"I want to be a good husband, Maura. I never want to do anything that will make you sorry you married me."

"I know that, soldier."

"And sometimes I'm going to need help. I don't mean I'll ever come home drunk and treat you bad or lay a hand on you, because I'm not that kind of a guy. But I don't know too much about getting along with people or trusting them. That's where I'll need you."

Maura gave his hand a reassuring squeeze. She stood on her toes and her lips brushed his cheek. "I'll be right here beside you, soldier, whatever happens."

The kid pushed himself back from the small kitchen table and sighed. He felt at peace with the world. "That's the best meal I ever ate."

Maura flushed with pleasure. "Farm girls are usually good cooks," she said, getting to her feet. She began to collect the dishes and carry them to the sink.

The kid stood up. "Can't I help?"

Maura shook her head. "No, you just sit back and relax."

"Okay, but it seems kind of funny being waited on. I'm not used to it."

"Doing the dishes is a girl's job."

"Speaking of jobs," the kid said, "I've been thinking about the kind of job I'd like to get."

Maura paused and arched her eyebrows questioningly, waiting for him to go on.

110

"I'm no white-collar guy," he said. "It's gotta be hard, tough work. I think I'll try the docks first. They tell me that if you're willing to hustle they pay pretty good. Would you mind having me do that kind of work?"

"No." The single word carried conviction. She wanted him to have a free hand in the selection but simultaneously to understand that this was so because she respected his personal choice and not because she was in the least indifferent to the type of employment he might seek.

He was gratified. The good feeling stole through him and this time he was not suspicious of it. Even the idea of responsibility, which only a few days before would have evoked angry contempt, he now found attractive. Because it would be accepted willingly, it could not be like being handcuffed.

"We're going to have to look for a place to live, too, in another few days," he said.

Her back was to him at the sink. "I know. It'll be fun looking."

"You got anything special in mind? Any particular kind of place or certain district?"

She turned, her hands soapy and the frilly apron contributing to her delightfully feminine appearance. "I'm not a big city girl, soldier, so I'd like to live at least far enough out to get away from the city's smelly exhaust fumes and all the racket."

"Me too."

This accord was intoxicating, and their businesslike talk assured them they were not irresponsibly romantic children only playing at a game of marriage.

"There is one more thing," she said.

"What's that?" he asked.

"Wouldn't you like to have your sister Janey come and live with us?"

"Would you?"

"Yes." Her head bobbed emphatically.

"Do you think she'd want to?"

"I'm sure she would and I'd love to have her."

"Then it's settled," he said.

"I love you, soldier," she said and blew a soapbubble kiss at him.

"And that makes me the luckiest guy in the world," he said, not glibly, after a pause.

He watched and marveled at her as she rinsed and wiped the dishes. The task completed, she remarked, smiling, "I now

111

make a motion that we adjourn this meeting, husband mine, and take a walk in the moonlight."

"I second that motion," he grinned.

Their bare feet slapping softly in the wet sand, they strolled along the deserted stretch of beach, laughing often, talking animatedly, carrying their shoes. And the hour grew late. Yet only when it became cold and the moon went down, did time again figure in their lives.

Maura shivered deliciously and yawned as sea water curled around her slim ankles and then frothily receded. "Soldier," she said, "it's time for us to go home."

He nodded pensively—and a shadow seemed to cross his face.

"A penny for your thoughts."

He said seriously, in a voice so solemn that it startled her, "I was thinking about us, Maura, and . . . " The words trailed off embarrassedly.

"Yes?" she prompted.

"I don't know how to say it."

"Try," she urged.

"Well," he said, struggling to find the right words to make her understand, "we're supposed to make our marriage final now and . . . " Again the awkward silence.

And briefly the unity was broken. They stood looking at one another helplessly.

Tonelessly she whispered, "Do you mean . . . you don't . . . want to?"

"Oh, God!" he groaned, for that wasn't what he meant at all. How could he explain? Desperately now he searched for the words that would bring them back together again, silently cursing his ineptness.

"Can't you see?" he said urgently, impulsively. "It's that you're a good girl."

She shook her head and blinked back tears. "I don't see." She was perplexed. Did he mean, could he possibly mean, that he didn't want a good girl?

"Oh, God," he said again, reading her thoughts. Caught in an emotional maze, this time he couldn't say to hell with it; this time he couldn't hide behind his anger. He couldn't reject. *Give love a chance!* She'd begged him to do that, with a woman's intuitive wisdom, and he wanted to. He wanted to love her and protect her and make her happy. But it

112

wasn't so much a question of burning want as it was one of viselike conditioning.

"I'm scared to go to bed with you," he blurted, knowing how crude and blunt was his language.

Now she was lost and hurt, frightened. The gulf between them widened dangerously. He was so strange, so unpredictable. But one word came through to her, like the urgent SOS from a ship fighting hopelessly against the storm-ravaged sea. It told her of his great need of her even as he was seemingly rejecting her. That word was "scared." Fear was something he would rather die than admit feeling. Indeed, it was questionable if he knew what it meant to be afraid when confronted by violence or mortal peril or death itself. Yet wrenched from his lips had been the admission that fear, or confusion disguised as fear, was the mocking intruder presently seeking to turn their first night of marriage into a nightmare.

"Why, soldier?" she asked. When he remained dumb, she went on, determined to bring them somehow back together and indissolubly make them one, "Don't you think I'm the one who should be afraid?"

"You?" The novelty of the possibility that this might be the case diverted attention away from himself. Why should she be afraid?

She explained. Because, she said in effect, the chaste young bride traditionally brings to the marriage bed her shy, imaginative fears of the experience when love first finds physical expression. But this does not mean that she fears sex itself or thinks that it is ugly or wrong or a bad thing to which, hiding her distaste, she must submit. It simply means that she is woman. And being woman, she is confident that, if her husband is a mature and gentle man, her life will be enriched, not shamed or burdened, by this act that transforms her from maid to future mother.

So, whatever her momentary doubts, she willingly goes to the arms of her mate, her love and yearning for fulfillment as a woman more than a match for her virgin's fears. And the proudest gift she can make her husband is, paradoxically, the basis for her fear, her virginity.

Thus, without fully grasping her strange, young-old husband's keen reluctance to consummate their marriage, she had shyly supplied him with the philosophical weapons with which to rout that reluctance. Heretofore he had not been able to associate sex with love and creativity, doubting even

113

the existence of the latter. Too indelibly stamped upon his mind had been the compulsive, vicious uses to which his hated old man had put sex. In his old man's hands it had been little more than an instrument of degradation and pathological dominance. Then, in reform school, he had witnessed its workings as an *agent provocateur* of violence and unspeakable perversions. And to him personally it had meant, at best, little more than a brief physiological release from tension.

Never before, even with the amoral Frankie, had it held out a promise of meaningful sharing. As a result, he had been afraid that to accept Maura's gift of herself would be to rob her of something and leave her soiled, and this terrible fear had immobilized him and tied his tongue. But now he perceived that, loving her as he did and having that love reciprocated, he had been wrong. He had had his eyes in the gutter rather than in the heavens. Truth was not always sordid or brutalizing. The revelation caused relief to flood through him and kindled a passion unrelated to lust.

"I'd never thought about it like that before," he admitted, and then she was in his arms. The last barrier between them was down. . . .

The kid awoke suddenly some time after dawn. He'd had a horrible dream, an insane, kaleidoscopic nightmare in which his long-dead, hell-haunted old man had figured evilly, and hordes of screaming gooks with blazing guns, and "Whispering Annie" and a parole officer named Warden, among others. Together these living and dead enemies had conspired successfully to steal Maura from him; they had forcibly whisked her away and then they had laughed at him and at his fear and frenzy when he had been unable to find her.

Now, his pulse pounding, he was fully awake, and Maura lay peacefully at his side, unthreatened, unmolested. He exhaled audibly in relief and looked at her with a mixture of awe and adoration. Her hair a disheveled cloud, her oddly pretty features relaxed contentedly in sleep, she appeared to him then to be the most beautiful and marvelous of creatures, a compassionate goddess who had halted his angry march to—or through—hell and who had led him back to the sunlight.

Here surely was a miracle, he thought.

114

Chapter Sixteen

JANEY HAD COME to live with them. It was a happy time in their lives. The kid had a steady job stevedoring; he settled down. The hard work was a purgative: as long as he kept at it the violence had no chance to build up, or the tension either. At first the guys who worked with him misunderstood. They thought he was trying to impress the big boys and get to the top too fast. They didn't like it. He felt their hostility.

"You're making the rest of us look bad," one of them told him. "Why don't you slow down?"

"I can't."

"What kinda screwy talk is that?"

"The truth. You've heard of people that got something wrong with their heads—they call it epilepsy—and unless they keep taking medicine they have fits, haven't you?"

"Sure, they gotta take goof balls. I read it in a magazine somewheres. But what's that got to do with you?"

"Well," the kid said, lowering his voice, "I don't go around broadcasting this, but I got something wrong with my head, too, in a way of speaking. When I work like hell and keep myself worn out, I'm okay. I can go along without any trouble. But when I take it easy, then something begins to go wrong with my head. It starts to fill up with funny ideas and I get pretty damned touchy. After that, the next thing I know I'm pitching a real bitch, raising all kinds of hell. So, since I'm trying to make it as just another Joe, I keep busy and I don't bother anybody, see?" The kid grinned.

"Yeah, sure," the other said, grinning back in a sickly way. There was something terrifying about the kid's grin and an unmistakable warning in the seemingly casual words: *Don't give me a bad time! Don't push me!*

The word was circulated. "This work-simple new guy is an oddball but he's okay. He ain't lookin' for a soft berth and he ain't no ass-kisser. He just wants to be left alone."

A gorilla-shaped, not-too-bright dock flunky called Punchy wasn't content to let it go at that. "There's somethin' phony about that kid," he mumbled. "I'm goin' to find out what is is." Punchy's ways could hardly be classsified as subtle. He stopped the kid the next time he met him. "Hey," he said. "Yeah, you. Who the hell do you think you're tryin' to impress?"

"Look," the kid said, "give us both a break and get out of my face. Fast!"

The other guys were watching, listening.

"Nobody talks to me like that," Punchy said, rolling toward the kid belligerently.

The kid grinned. *I guess I gotta do it,* he thought. In the same fraction of a second he sidestepped and set himself. Punchy never saw the short right hand that knocked the wind out of him and dumped him on the seat of his pants. Still, there he was on the deck, gasping for air, his eyes protruding slightly from their sockets.

The kid grinned down at him. "I think we ought to be able to get along fine from here on."

They did. That right hand was language Punchy understood. The kid worked all the harder. Nobody minded. He had been accepted as one of the guys.

When Maura shyly told him one night that she was pregnant, the kid thought he would burst with an uncocky pride. Who would ever have believed it possible? Here was that tough, violent youngster from reform school everybody had predicted would wind up in the electric chair now a square, a working stiff, a married guy whose wife was going to have a baby. And he was happy, really happy. This was the life! He marveled at the miraculous thing that had happened to him and believed Maura when she told him it always would be like this.

But a storm was gathering.

It broke suddenly when a jurisdictional row between rival unions, one of them gangster dominated, erupted at the docks where the kid worked. When this struggle flared into the open, with the gangster-controlled union making an all-out bid to crush its lawful rival, there was a strike, name-calling, trouble, then violence.

Inevitably, though he tried to avoid it, the kid was drawn into the violence. There were a couple of shifty characters in his union, minor officials in the local, who had been bought out. At a meeting of the rank and file they preached capitulation. What's the advantage, they argued, of ending up crippled for life or worse? What chance did they, all of them, have of bucking an organized setup that had the political fix in and the power of an army behind them?

"I'll tell you smart bastards what chance," the kid said, getting to his feet. As soon as he stood up, the gangster's planted hecklers began hooting and giving him a bad time. He told them to go to hell. The honest majority shouted down the paid hecklers and demanded that the kid be allowed to speak his piece. His blunt words and crazy courage put new fight into the members. They overwhelmingly voted down a motion to merge—and thereby give in—to their rivals.

Three of the gangster's enforcers met the kid after the meeting. They had a proposition. "Join us," he was told, "and you're made. You'll go places. The boss likes guys with guts. But he don't like being bucked and it ain't healthy to buck him. Know what I mean?"

"Yeah," the kid said. "I know what you mean. And I know what you can tell your big phony of a boss. You can tell him to go to hell. I don't do business with snakes."

The trio got tough.

The kid got tougher.

He beat the three enforcers insensible with his bare hands almost before they could get the saps out of their back pants pockets. It was the only answer the kid knew for degraded, ruthless men who sought to coerce and dominate with threats and violence. Odd, how finally it was his anger as a working stiff that trapped him. His anger had triggered the violence, and at that point hate took over, his savage ability to use his hands had put him in an impossible position.

The peaceful, useful pattern of his life was shattered. Common sense urged him to leave before it was too late, to go quickly somewhere else with Maura and Janey and start over. But hate jeered at common sense. Hate asked him if he'd lost his nerve, his guts. "Fight the bastards!" hate demanded. "Fight them or admit you've turned yellow!"

Sure, the gangster union boss would retaliate. He had to, to save face. If he didn't move swiftly to crush the kid he'd be laughed out of town. All this the kid knew too well. And it was little consolation to be able to tell himself he was in the right. Actually, it wasn't a question of right or wrong. It was a question of survival.

117

The kid walked the streets, his mind in chaos. His legs kept moving and time passed. An hour. Two. Then he phoned Maura. He'd talk it over with her and Janey. He'd ask them what they thought. But the time for discussion had passed.

"Don't come home, soldier!" Maura cried out after he had identified himself. "They're here!"

The kid heard the sound of a blow. He heard his wife moan.

"We're waitin' for ya, tough guy," an ugly voice said. "Ya better come fast and alone or you know what." The words were punctuated with a low, sadistic chuckle.

Ya better come fast and alone or you know what. Or they would take their hate out on Maura. They would get at him through her. Perhaps through Janey, too.

"I'll be there," the kid said. "Alone."

The kid, however, didn't go alone. He took hate with him.

They were waiting for him, a masked, pistol-carrying and blackjack and pipe-wielding goon squad: five big guys and a smaller one to bark the orders and do the thinking. As he stepped through the front door, he was smashed across the face with an open hand that left a livid imprint on one cheek. He'd expected that.

"You didn't have brains enough to lay off, did you, punk?" the small one said. He was the chuckler, a movie and TV stereotype of the undersized tough guy, who wore built-up shoes, and slicked his black hair down like a latter-day Valentino. In his fist he held a .45 automatic. "Well, before we're through with you you'll know the boss means business."

"Yeah," chimed in the hulking and hairy Neanderthal man who obviously stooged for the small dandy, "we're gonna take you for a little ride."

A ride meant a bad dumping, a working over and probably a few broken bones, with a scalp massage thrown in for good measure, but it didn't mean lights out and getting tossed into the bay in the middle of a cement slab—unless, that is, you got frisky and failed to submit to the therapy.

Maura was deathly afraid that if they took her now granite-faced husband away she would never see him again. These men were beasts. They mustn't be allowed to take him.

"No," she protested. "No!" She wrenched free from the big goon holding her. He grabbed for her and she snatched the mask from his face, raking her fingernails from his forehead to his chin. He cursed and struck her viciously in the abdomen, where she was heavy with the child.

Janey screamed.

The kid had stood transfixed. In that instant he went berserk. Snarling, he made for the big ape who had struck Maura. Quickly the others moved in on him. He was black-jacked, piped, and pistol-whipped savagely. Finally he fell and they put the boots to him. Janey tried to intervene and was slammed to the floor. Maura dragged herself across the room and, in an effort to protect him, sought to throw her body over his. She was kicked aside. A sadistic chuckle filled the room.

In the distance a siren wailed; a neighbor had telephoned the police. The goons and the dandy left in a hurry. Their night's work was done.

Bloody from head to foot, sick and vomiting, barely conscious, the kid got to his feet and reeled to the front door just as the squad car answering the call bucked to a halt outside. "Get an ambulance quick," he said. "My wife's hurt bad."

Twenty-five minutes later Maura was wheeled into surgery. She remained there over two hours, while, with Janey and the elderly pastor, the kid kept a grim vigil in a nearby waiting room. He refused medical attention for himself and angrily brushed aside the questions of the pair of detectives assigned to investigate the assault.

"Dammit," the kid said curtly, "don't bother me now."

"We're only trying to do our job," the dicks told him in bored, patient voices.

"Yeah, I know. I've heard that song before." The kid had never forgotten or forgiven a big detective named Mulligan.

One of the dicks persisted. "You wouldn't want these hoodlums to go unpunished, would you?"

The kid laughed harshly. "Don't worry, copper, they won't. I'll see that they get theirs if I have to chase the bastards all the way to hell to do it."

"That's a job for the police and the courts. Now, if you'll just tell us everything you know about . . ."

The color had been draining from the kid's bruised and bloody face. His eyes began to glitter dangerously. "Take a walk, copper. Do us both a favor and don't bother me with any more questions until I know how Maura is going to be."

"Do you mean to tell me you don't intend to co-operate with us?" the dick demanded, offended, implying threats.

"Put it any way you want. But get the hell away from me or we're going to have trouble."

The dick started to swell up with indignation at this affront to his badge. He opened his mouth to put the kid in his place when his brother officer led him off to a corner of the room. "We'll talk to him later."

The kid's rage subsided. What the bulls needed was a new script writer, he thought. Always they fed you the same old line. *Co-operate. Papa Authority knows best. Tell us all about it. That's a job for us.* Maybe they were right. That didn't make what they said any more palatable. Less, in fact, because smugness gave the words fat bellies.

Invariably, on contact, he antagonized authority; and authority antagonized him. Again in this new crisis they were at loggerheads. Whose fault this was didn't matter. Now only Maura mattered.

Maura was his life. "She's *got* to be okay!" he said, smashing his right fist into his left palm for emphasis. But she wasn't okay; she was dying, and there was nothing the surgeons could do to save her. It was a miracle they were able to save the child, a boy. From her ruptured womb, by Caesarean section, they lifted the wrinkled infant, blew air into its lungs, patted its behind, fought dedicatedly until a weak wail came from its lips. Into an incubator it then went, with a fifty-fifty chance of survival, and the nurse who carried it wept because she knew its unconscious young mother, almost a child herself, would never cuddle and croon to and love this tiny boy baby. Maura was in shock and hemorrhaging. The big goon's blows and kicks had burst the peritoneum as well as the womb.

Later one of the doctors showed the kid his new son and told him, "We were fortunately able to deliver the child. I believe it will live. But your wife hasn't much time. She's conscious now and asking for you. Spare her as much as possible, son."

Maura lived only a few hours. They were the most terrible hours in the kid's life. After borrowing a clean shirt and washing the blood from his battered face, the kid spent what little time remained at Maura's bedside. He held her small, cold hand, his face betraying none of his inner agony.

"I just saw the baby," he said and added some traditional banalities he thought would make her happy: "The little

120

guy's fine, only he sure is noisy and I'm afraid he's going to look like me." He grinned. "Because he was born early they got him in some kind of oxygen box," he explained.

Yes, sure, he added, answering her question, she'd be able to hold him darned soon. "And now I suppose I'll have to learn how to put those three-cornered pants on him." Maura smiled and he kept talking. "Of course I'm fine. Just a few cuts, knots, and bumps on this thick head of mine." Nothing worth a second thought. "And the doc tells me that you'll be good as new in nothing flat."

The future belonged to them and it would be a good future. Yes, you're darned right, there'd be brothers and sisters for their little guy. And . . . The kid talked on, while his heart and mind screamed silently in protest, while he almost fainted from the effects of the terrible beating he had taken.

"I'm so happy, soldier," Maura said. "And I love you so much." She smiled again and closed her eyes. Then she sighed softly.

The smile remained.

"She's dead," the doctor said.

I killed her! the kid thought. "Oh, God, I killed her!" he cried out. He should never have returned to the restaurant a second time. He had known better and yet, selfishly, out of his need, he had done so. In returning, he had signed Maura's death warrant.

He leaped to his feet, wild-eyed. Tongues of fire reached out and enveloped him. Consciousness was consumed in the flame and smoke of the inferno. The tormented cries beating against his mind grew fainter, fainter. He revolved wildly in the fiery center of this spiritual Gehenna. All sense of time was gone, and identity. And this time agony, for him a slut who embraced him with indecent fervor, was not his companion. This time he was agony, its essence.

They managed to subdue him with force. They gave him a powerful sedative. For two weeks, watched and attended twenty-four hours a day, he raved insanely, obscenely. He screamed, cursed, cried. With a strength that was more than human, he strained against the physical restraints and the nurses and doctors who sought to keep him from injuring himself in his madness.

Meanwhile Maura was buried and Janey bravely carried on. Maura's tragic death momentarily aroused the city. In a burst of civic indignation the power of the gangster-dominated

121

union was smashed. Through an informer, the police learne
the names of the goons who had attacked the kid and Maur
Indictments were returned by the grand jury against then
Three were arrested; one—the small, laughing one—w
killed resisting arrest (he didn't get his hands up fast enoug
and made what the police called a "menacing" move)
Maura's killer had fled.

As abruptly as the shock of his young wife's death ha
robbed the kid of his grip on reality, he became ration
again. Hate finally had penetrated his torment and clampe
an iron hand on his mind. Physically exhausted by his ma
struggles, hoarse from screaming and cursing, his thought
nevertheless were cold and clear. He grinned disarmingly
the nurses, the internes, the doctors, and apologized fc
having been such a problem. He acted profoundly gratefu
when told the baby had lived.

He had Janey bring a lawyer with her when she visite
him and arranged for her to take temporary custody of th
tiny boy and to turn over all his property and money t
her. The money was what he and Maura had saved fc
the baby and the future. Janey was reluctant to accept
at first, fearing that to do so would help the kid to cut himse
free from all his responsibilities and send him away rudde
less, full of bitterness and hate and anger. Wasn't it bes
she asked, out of the kid's hearing, that he be left with som
responsibilities? The question was answered in the negativ
and she finally agreed after both the lawyer and the kid
doctor, as well as a psychiatrist from the VA who had bee
called in for consultation, said it would be the wisest cours
"His mind is not well," they told her, "and he may requir
hospitalization for some time to come. This will obvia
any questions arising as to his competence in connection wit
the child or his property and funds." The necessary pape
were drawn up and executed.

Now he was a pauper and he had signed away all leg
right to custody of his son. "But can I see him?" he asked.

"Certainly," he was assured. This was regarded as a goo
sign.

When they brought the infant, Janey accompanying then
he thought: *Hey, he actually does look something like me!* H
was no longer red and wrinkled and puny-looking. He w
now a laughing "brute" of six pounds. And he was part
Maura; that was what counted most. For a few moments th

122

two were left alone and during that period the kid whispered to his tiny son in a voice barely audible, "I'll get even for both of us. It'll be up to you to get ahead."

The next day the elderly pastor visited the kid. He was kind, tactful. "I've been praying for you," he said.

"Pray for Maura, Reverend," the kid replied. "I don't rate anybody's prayers. It's my fault she's dead." He could face that fact calmly now and doggedly resist every effort made to disprove it.

The kid willingly talked with the two detectives handling the case. "Sure," he lied, "I'll be glad to be a witness against the dogs that gave Maura and me the business." He lulled the detectives' doubts and they told him what they knew about the big goon still at large. It was useful information.

One morning his doctor asked him casually, "You know, don't you, that you'll have to be held here another thirty days for observation?"

The kid knew how loaded the question was. And after that thirty days there might be too many more months and years at a VA hospital. "That's okay." He accompanied the bland lie with a smile and a shrug. He was wholly agreeable—on the surface. And he waited patiently. Hospital personnel relaxed their vigilance. The kid stole the key to the storeroom, got his clothes, dressed and escaped.

He went straight to his wife's grave. Janey, believing that she was indulging him, had told him precisely where in the cemetery it was located. "I'm sorry, Maura," he said aloud. Then he looked at the heavens. "It should have been me," he told the sky. In that moment all human warmth left him. Maura was dead and all his hopes were buried here with her.

He had a job to do.

Chapter Seventeen

WITH THE CUNNING of a hunted and hunting, hounded and hounding wild animal, the kid dodged the police, who had put out a flyer on him. They thought he was a psycho. They wanted to take him back into protective custody. "Use caution in apprehending," the flyer said. "Subject may be armed and should be regarded as extremely dangerous."

The kid saw the flyer and then a follow-up APB. He laughed. It *was* funny. It was funny as hell. The only time in his life he had been armed was the time when he was in the Army. Uncle Sam had given him an automatic rifle and he had used it to kill gooks. Killing gooks, little guys half a world away, had been all right. The more the better. They didn't put you in jail for it; they gave you medals. Shooting bandy-legged little bastards in a Korean rice field was all very legal. They came at you, full of life and hopped-up bravery, their bellies full or half full or a quarter full of rice, millet, and maybe dog, their wiry bodies encased in ill-fitting, sacklike uniforms, their war boots tennis shoes, and you got them in your sights and squeezed the trigger. You kept on sighting and squeezing. That was all there was to it. You didn't even have to think. It didn't matter how you felt about killing them, whether you liked it or hated it, or whether you felt nothing at all. Just fight, fight where and when and how you were told, and everything would be fine. You might even end up a hero. When you returned home, they'd play a band for you and good-looking gals would be dancing on the docks. Provided, of course, you didn't return home in a box, a stiff. But what the hell! If that happened you would be a hero for sure. So you couldn't lose.

But now it was different. This wasn't Korea; this was the U.S.A. There wasn't a war on, or even a police action. And you were a civilian, not a soldier. Goons were your enemies, not gooks. The substitution of an *n* for a *k* made the difference. It was worth thinking about: the government got into a beef with another government that was trying to snatch territory and subjugate people with force, and you and a lot of guys like you were given a gun and told to get with it. You got with it. Then you came home, married a girl, and settled down. You didn't want any trouble. But trouble came looking for you and you refused to run. Some gangster bastard was trying to take over the union you belonged to. He was using goons as the North Koreans and the Chinese Reds had used soldiers. But it wasn't legal to shoot them full of holes, not even after one of the whoresons hit and kicked your wife to death. No, you were supposed to leave it to the police. Goons had rights. Gangsters did, too. They had rights which said you had no right to settle the beef yourself. You couldn't take the law into your own hands, they said; and this was what a prosecutor once had told a jury when he tried your mother.

You didn't understand the legalisms. You didn't even try to. Nor did you try to convince yourself that you really were in the right. There wasn't any need to rationalize. You had a job to do and, right or wrong, you intended to do it. Yes, and you knew that doing the job could get you thrown into jail for a long time. You examined that fact, without anger, before forgetting it. You didn't intend to go to jail if you could help it. But the legions of hell couldn't lock you up until your job was done. Then you'd take your chances on the outcome.

Jail wasn't your biggest worry. What really scared the hell out of you was the chance your mind would crumble. It was working okay at the moment but doubt nagged at you and a voice warned you to hurry. *Hurry!* Get the job done!

Your brain was like a spotlight. It was a spotlight that couldn't be adjusted, though. It threw its burning light straight ahead only. The sides were in darkness. You could see nothing there or behind. So you stopped looking in any direction but directly in front of you. Your eyes were dazzled by the unnatural brilliance of what you saw. And you moved fast, wondering always how long it would be before, with a splutter or without warning, the beam of light would die and the darkness would be everywhere, permanently. It would be then a time of terror far worse than being caged or dead.

The kid stayed in the city until, after scouring the waterfront dives, he got a lead to the man he was after, the goon who had beat and kicked Maura. "Pete Briz oughtta know if anybody does," he was told.

A young wharf rat, Pete Briz, it turned out, did know, but he wasn't very talkative at first.

"Beat it. Scram."

The kid laughed.

"What's the matter, you hard of hearing? I said take it on the Arthur."

"Not until you talk."

"I ain't talking. Now get out of my room or I throw you out."

"It don't work that way," the kid said. "It don't work that way at all, Pete. You tell me where I can find this bastard or I kill you right now, nice and slow."

Full of bravado, Briz said, "I wouldn't tell you the right time."

He took a step forward; so did the kid. They stood facing each other. Briz glared at the death mask that was the kid's face, at the cold gray-green eyes that stared back unblinkingly. The kid's hand was a blur of movement. The open-handed slap snapped the other's head back.

"Talk!"

Pete Briz knew fear and fear goaded him to make a mistake. He pulled a switchblade knife and made a lunge for the kid. The kid's right hand drove into his mouth like a pile driver. The kid kicked the knife aside and looked down at Briz.

"You ready to start talking?"

Pete Briz nodded, whined, and spit out teeth. He was ready to talk, more than ready. It was of no consequence that his speech was thick and bloody.

Less than twenty-four hours later, grinning as Death must grin, the kid walked into another water-front dive just across the state line and confronted the man he was after. His man—the goon's name was Blaze—was a big, arrogant ham-fisted ex-pug with a thick-lipped face and close-set eyes. The hairline began hardly more than an inch and a half above those eyes.

Blaze was at the bar with a couple of pals and a peroxide blonde with an overpainted face. He was drunk, and his raucous laughter filled the room. Here, obviously, he was a big wheel, an operator.

The kid stood just inside the swinging doors, giving his eyes a chance to adjust to the darker interior. The spot light that was his brain grew brighter; its light was white and searing. He wanted, passionately, to kill Blaze. Not swiftly and mercifully but slowly and terribly. It took all his will power to keep from throwing himself at him, this phony, two-legged animal who had killed Maura, who had robbed him of his last hope for a future. And there the laughing sonofabitch sat, pawing the blonde, putting on a big front for his two scummy pals.

"Blaze." He said the name softly.

"Huh?" Blaze grunted, turning.

The place quieted. Every pair of eyes in the dive focused on the kid. Blaze gave a gasp of recognition. A vein on his forehead began to throb.

"I came all by myself, Blaze," the kid said. "I didn't even tell the bulls I knew where you were. Because this is something strictly between you and me, isn't it, Blaze?"

"I don't know what you're talking about," Blaze said, dry-mouthed, tensed.

"Then you got a short memory or you're a goddamned liar."

"You must've made some mistake," Blaze said, managing a sickly smile.

"No, Blaze," the kid said, shaking his head, "I didn't make the mistake. You did. You made it when you were so stupid you didn't think I'd look you up. When you started to run, Blaze, you should've kept running. That way you might've stayed ahead of me for a while."

"Wait a minute," the blonde said. "What's this all about, anyway?"

The kid told her. He told her about Maura and the baby. He didn't mention himself and the dumping he'd taken.

"I read about that," the blonde said. "It was awful," she added. She turned and demanded of Blaze if the kid's accusation was true.

"Shut up," Blaze said. "Keep your nose out of my business."

"You see," the kid said. "You see how tough this bastard is with women?"

"You're crazy," Blaze growled. He snatched a whisky bottle and broke the bottom off against the bar. Gripped by the neck, its sharp, jagged edges made a formidable weapon.

The kid hadn't moved. "Yeah, Blaze, you're right," he said quietly. "I'm crazy. I'm so crazy I'm willing to spot you the bottle."

127

"You ain't got a chance," Blaze said. "If you push me I'll get you."

"You got it the wrong way around, Blaze. I'm here to get you, and I'll kill anybody that tries to interfere." The kid took a step forward and glared briefly at first one and then the other of Blaze's companions.

"Deal me out," the shorter one said.

"Yeah," the other said, "this ain't our beef."

Blaze came off the bar stool, breathing heavily. The kid took another step toward him. A distance of not more than four feet separated the two men. "It's your move, Blaze," the kid said, and Blaze began to curse. A stream of obscenities poured from his lips. Suddenly he lunged and swiped murderously at the kid with the bottle.

The kid had been ready. Blaze didn't fare so well. First he lost his bottle and then he almost lost his life. The kid's iron fists repeatedly smashed into his body and face. While this happened the spotlight turned from white to red, its crimson glow robbing the kid of volition.

Blaze, a broken hulk now, had fallen to the floor and was covering his bloody, pulpy face with his hands.

"I've had enough!" he moaned.

The kid laughed harshly, the death grin still on his face. The uncontrollable urge to kill had passed. There was the taste of wormwood to his revenge. It had given him no satisfaction, no release from the fearful tension. The primary guilt still was his; it always would be. Violence never would be able to change that.

He kicked Blaze under the chin and walked out. That last exaggerated act of brutality had been necessary. It kept the relationship of the two men in balance. It proved no more though, than a period at the end of a sentence: the end termination. When he reached the curb he began to vomit. He broke out in a cold sweat. His legs were made of rubber. He was physically ill, but he knew the illness would pass.

There was something Blaze hadn't known. From the first time the kid had seen him, when Maura had ripped the mask from his ugly face, Blaze had reminded the kid of his old man, even had strongly resembled him both in physical appearance and in his actions. Inevitably then, during their violent encounter, the kid had found a way to get back at that despised father image. (That in part explained why later, he had walked into Larson's Gym and polished off

128

Angelo. His pathological hate for his old man had been transferred in that moment to all fighters.)

You gotta be able to take it!

That's what his old man had shouted. If you couldn't take it, you were in a bad way. You were vulnerable, a weak-sister fool, the prisoner of a fiendish torturer whose soft voice spoke to you mockingly even as he stretched you on his emotional rack. The pain was more than you could bear.

Well, by God, he could take it. He'd show the whole goddamned world he could take it. And while he was at it he could let hate drive him—straight to hell. That, he figured, was probably where he belonged in any event. Either there or oblivion, the place that didn't exist for souls without existence. Denied even the pleasure of pain and regret, they were the anomalies of the universe: imperfect, driven things which had no hope of heaven and no fear of hell; whose only fear was that they might reveal their weakness, blind to the fact that this "weakness" was a strength.

The kid drifted. He worked as a powder monkey and at a dozen other dangerous jobs, time and again insanely risking his life, tempting death, virtually wooing death. He sent Janey most of the money he earned but never gave a return address. He never stayed in one place long. He never formed any close relationships.

He lived with violence. He had to. He wanted to. Violence kept the spotlight burning. Without it, the light would go out and he would be only a mindless, animated corpse, going nowhere, without purpose, without plan. Yet with it, paradoxically, he had to sell his humanity, his sense of belonging. He had to grin and walk alone. He could never be a father to his small son.

It would be a brief and terrible life.

Chapter Eighteen

"WELL, MISTER," the kid said, "that's about it."

There was a life, its ugliness, its savagery, its violence. And its tragedy. There it was, without apology, a frightening thing. But not without meaning, not without value. Unsubtle, yes, but ironical, too. Curiously so.

I had to be especially careful now, with this abrupt return to the present. The transition might be difficult, tricky. It could be impossible. It depended upon whether one reality could be linked to another. I thought it could.

Casually I asked the kid where he'd been since that day he'd walked into Larson's Gym. He told me with a carnival fighting in one of those setups where the rube is given twenty-five dollars if he can last three rounds. He'd been fired—for inciting a riot when he'd given a small southern town's boxing hero a particularly brutal pasting. The rubes had almost lynched him and had torn the carnival apart.

"Mister," he said dryly, "I almost started another Civil War." He grinned, looking at me sharply, almost defiantly. The quip helped hide the exposed wound.

I grinned back. My grin told him I wasn't staring like a country bumpkin at its festering rawness. A man's wounds, physical, mental, or spiritual, my look said, did not positively put him in the category of side-show freak.

You looked with neither fascination nor repulsion, only recognition. You distinguished between a saccharine sympathy and a concerned empathy. And you wondered: Can the wound be healed? Can the pain be allayed? You didn't think in terms of moral imperatives. You didn't recoil in righteous horror. You didn't cast verbal stones or invective. Nor did you pretend to know with certainty the will of Almighty God.

I asked the kid what his plans for the future were.

"Plans?" the kid said, genuinely puzzled. "Hell, mister, I don't have any plans. I'll just keep on taking it and dishing it out until I can't take it or dish it out any longer." Then, he told me, he'd be through. (Then he'd be dead, cold, stone dead.) He said he didn't think he had much further to go.

He was probably right—and he didn't care. His pain and guilt were that intensely felt, and yet he couldn't admit the presence of either, even to himself. He couldn't say, simply, "I'm lost, mister, and sick and mixed-up." He had to simplify and externalize. He had to keep driving himself further and further into that inferno called violence.

"I'm also trying to tell you," Dr. Tom Layton had said, "that I'm afraid the kid is under a sentence of death." My psychiatrist friend had let me discover for myself why, unconsciously or subconsciously, the death sentence had been self-imposed.

Primarily as a penance. An unworded *mea culpa*!

Secondarily as the fulfillment of a need and as a destructive "solution" to an insoluble problem, in the manner of one who, confounded by the concept of a mathematical infinity, seeks to solve Zeno's paradox of the race between Achilles and a tortoise by booby-trapping the tortoise.

I lit the fuse. It was that or give up, admit defeat. I heard my own voice. It could have belonged to a stranger; in a way, it did. "What about your mother, son? And Maura? If they're looking down, what do you think they think about you now? You're hardly a specimen they can be proud of."

From the kid's throat came the fear-and-hurt cry of a wild animal that has felt the sudden, cruel bite of the jaws of a steel trap. Hate and pain burned in the kid's eyes. His right hand shot out, the fingers closing on my shirt and coat.

"Damn you!" he snarled. "Forget about them, see!"

"Sure, son, sure," I said. "It was a stupid thing to ask. I apologize."

"You mean that or are you just talking words?"

"I mean it."

I meant I apologized, that I was sorry I had to say what I did.

The kid relaxed his grip; his knuckle-smashed hand fell to his side. "All right, mister," he said guardedly. "Now you know about me; you know the whole story. You know I'm no damned good and if you got any sense you know that there's nothing you or anybody can do about it. So what's your proposition?"

Not yet, I thought. *Not until he's had a few hours to think over my questions.*

"It's getting late," I said. "What do you say we talk it over

131

tomorrow morning?" I took two ten-dollar bills from my wallet, handed them to the kid, and asked him to be at my place the next morning early, giving him my address and directions how to get there.

"We'll talk business then. Okay?"

"Okay."

As soon as I reached my apartment I called Dr. Tom Layton. He had said he would be waiting for a call.

"Tom?"

"Yes."

"This is Charley. I just left the kid. I'm to see him again in the morning."

"How did it go?"

I told him. Not pleasantly. Ruggedly. Brutally. That was how it had gone.

"Yet you're determined to go through with it?"

"More than ever."

"It's dangerous."

"Sure. So is the hydrogen bomb."

Tom Layton understood; the analogy originally had been his. We create lethal weapons (or personalities) and invariably are then appalled by our creations. Foolishly, tragically, we satisfy ourselves that we have done our duty and convinced ourselves that we are blameless by righteously denouncing as evil and proscribed what we personally, by action or inaction, have brought into being.

Well, I wasn't satisfied. And as I climbed tiredly into bed I didn't feel very righteous or blameless.

Again, rolling and tossing, my mind insisted on functioning, on creating thought patterns and images, long after the physical and mental machine cried for rest. After a time I slipped into a kind of twilight state between sleep and wakefulness. I thought how the newspapers and the public had appropriated a diagnostic label and, in their moral zeal, applied it to those who outraged them most, the psychologically demon-driven psychopaths. It came to me forcefully how true were Tom Layton's words: "In short, Charley, I don't believe that ignorance, even righteous and pious ignorance, however well-intentioned, is the best judge of evil; nor do I believe that it is a competent weapon to oppose evil."

Psychopathic personalities were not forged and they did not overtly find expression in a vacuum. To assert (which solemn folly) that they were and did was the equivalent of claiming that when a bomb explodes, "blame" must be fixed

132

exclusively on the bomb itself. Yet most people would call the kid evil, criminal. They would see in him evidence of the displeasure of heaven and the cunning of hell. They would want him locked up, punished. They would say, crudely, that what had happened to him offered no excuse for his becoming the sort of person he was. They would insist on fixing responsibility because it was unthinkable for them not to do so. They would mitigate his blame only, and then grudgingly, by finding him wholly different, alien. They would be shocked and indignant if someone told them the same thing could have happened to them.

"Impossible!" they would snap. Or "It's a lie!"

Truth was what they said it was. Truth was their prisoner, just as the kid was hate's prisoner. The difference was that the impostor they called truth voluntarily remained in their "protective" custody, while the kid hated and resisted his jailer. Repeatedly and violently he sought to escape. Perhaps I could show him how. . . .

A long night passed; morning came. The kid's pounding on the door woke me. I got up, let him in, dressed, and then we drove over to the eatery where I had my meals. When we finished eating, I asked the kid point-blank if *he* wanted to be the light heavy champ.

"Me?" he asked incredulously.

"You," I said. "You've got the equipment: the guns and the guts."

The kid's laugh was derisive. "Mister, believe me, I wouldn't take it if you handed it to me on a silver platter."

He obviously meant what he said. He hated fighting and fighters, but he couldn't keep away from either. Fighting fighters—physical violence—was his brutal yardstick; it told him what he continually had to know: whether he could still take it, still dish it out. It let him externalize that terrible pathological hate. It kept him precariously bound to reality. And it permitted him to pay the prohibitive interest on the debt he thought he owed his dead young wife and his child.

"I didn't think you'd be interested," I said, finishing my coffee.

"Was *that* your proposition, mister?"

"No." It wasn't.

I told the kid all about Angelo and Mike McGuire and his dream. "They're good people, son."

133

"Yeah, sure," the kid said without rancor. "The damn world's full of good people. So what?"

"So I'd like to see Angelo champ. He and Mike deserve it."

The kid looked at me dubiously. "Hell, mister, get smart to yourself. Nobody *deserves* anything. I found that out a long time ago and you should've too. You got to be able to take what you want. And then you only got it as long as you can keep the other bums from snatching it away from you."

"Perhaps," I said. "But you figure you deserve revenge, don't you?"

The question caught the kid by surprise.

"Revenge against what?" he asked.

"The world. The fighting racket. Your old man."

The works. Even a savage keeper named hate.

The kid let this sink in. Then he grinned. "Yeah, mister, you're right. That's the only thing I do want and that I figure I got coming."

I told him bluntly how he could get it.

That was my proposition.

And when I got to the office I wrote a long letter—to Janey.

134

Chapter Nineteen

THAT AFTERNOON, after helping square the assault-and-battery charges against the kid, I was at Larson's Gym watching Angelo train and comparing him mentally with the champ. They were opposites. One had the classical face and build of a bronze Roman god; the other, an acromegalous face, at once both porcine and vulpine, and a hairy brute's body. It was this antipodean quality that fascinated me.

Angelo was young, not yet twenty-five; the champ was in his mid-thirties, old, very old for a fighter. Angelo had chosen boxing as another youngster might pick the law, say, or medicine; the champ had graduated—or gravitated—from street fights and barroom brawls. Angelo was a man and a gentleman; the champ was a coarse, crude character who had been in a hundred scrapes. But the champ was still the champ, and a savage slugger and mauler. He was like a big, tough grizzly bear—hard to beat. He'd held the title almost four years; he'd defended it successfully ten times.

The champ's manager and fat Joe Fisch, cigar in mouth, sauntered in as though they had just happened to be passing by and decided on the spur of the moment to drop in. (I'd been tipped they intended to put in an appearance.) They watched Angelo go a couple of rounds before they said anything. I wasn't surprised when they talked a title fight to Mike. They needed a substitute for the hospitalized Tiger Glade—and the Angel plainly was their boy. After they left, Mike acted like a woman about to have her first baby.

Dazed. Flustered. Happy. Confused. Excited. You name it.

Contracts for the scrap were inked in Joe Fisch's swank uptown offices, with the newspaper and publicity boys making a production of it. When they got around to posing the champ and the challenger, the champ took a dirty dig at Angelo.

"Be careful, pretty boy," the champ sneered. "Don't let that punk kid beat your face in again like he did Glade before I get a chance to do it. I hear he's still in town."

I put a warning hand on Angelo's shoulder. "Relax," I whispered. "You're about to see some fun."

Just then another voice said insolently, "Say, champ, you looking for a good sparring partner, maybe?"

The champ's big, thick head snapped around. "Who's this guy?"

"This guy, champ," I said with relish, "is 'that punk kid' you were just talking about. I thought you might want to meet him, so I asked him to come up here with me."

Sure, the champ knew he'd been put on the spot, but he was too cagey and vain to show it. He glared murderously at me and then told the kid, "You're the boy I been looking for."

"And now you found me," the kid said, smiling that weird smile. His gray-green eyes were full of cold mockery.

"Yeah," the champ said. "Now I found you." He didn't look exactly happy. I couldn't say I blamed him.

I got Borden on the phone and reported what had happened. "So now, General," I added smugly, "you got yourself another angle and some more hot sports copy."

Borden screamed, "but we've already put our sports final to bed! You told me to leave handling of the signing to you. All we gave it was straight coverage."

My name was Judas; first name Svengali. I'd let "The Rag" beat us to the story. Borden's pained curses and cries poured unmelodiously from the receiver. The little scoundrel really did blow his top when I made some clucking sympathy noises into the phone and advised him unctuously to watch his blood pressure.

When he had raved himself out of breath, I inquired casually, "By the way, General, have you read my day's column yet?"

He hadn't; he'd been too busy.

"Well, you'd better. It's all there, done up in one neat package."

"But how . . . ?"

"I got a crystal ball, too," I said, and hung up.

I drove Mike and Angelo home. On the way, Mike laughed himself to tears in recounting and mimicking the incident back in Joe Fisch's office. "Did you see it, Charley? Did you see that crazy expression on the champ's face when he had to take the kid on as a sparring partner and act like he liked it?"

I grinned. I'd seen it. (Hell, I'd stage-managed it.)

Angelo wasn't amused. He told us in so many words he didn't like any part of it.

Mike was incredulous.

"Why don't you like it, Angelo?" I asked.

"Because it looks to me as though this wise-guy kid is trying to make fools out of all of us."

"I don't think so," I said.

"Well, we'll see, Mr. Evans. We'll sure see."

It hurt me, but I had to do it. I'd gone this far. "What's the matter, Angelo? Worried? Afraid the kid might come back and want another piece of you?"

Angelo looked stricken. I'd hit him where it hurt, unexpectedly. He got a grip on himself. "Mr. Evans," he said with a quiet, cold ferocity, "I'm going to show you how worried or afraid I am."

Good boy, Angelo, I thought.

My words did what I'd hoped they would—they made Angelo fighting mad. Mad at everybody and everything. I never saw a fighter train so hard, with such dedicated concentration. I never saw a fighter so serious or so deadly. Mike watched his boy with awe, speechless for the first time in his voluble life.

Angelo obviously wasn't training only for the champ. There was something else, someone else. Involved wasn't so much a matter of getting even. It wasn't the idea that others might think he wasn't a man if he didn't boldly force the kid's hand now that he had the opportunity. It was more personal than that, more psychically cankerous. He had lost a measure of his self-respect, his integrity as a person, and there was only one way to regain what he had lost. Whatever doubts might beset him as to his ability to do so, however abrasive the memory of the beating and the humiliation, there was no escaping from total awareness what the result would be should he find himself not man enough for the task and the test.

He knew.

How ironically well he knew I was to discover later, at a crucial time.

The kid came to see me. After the first day's workout with the champ, he looked as though he had been run through a meat grinder. Grinning, he told me how he'd agitated the champ in front of the newspaper reporters and how the champ had tried to kill him when they had mixed it up in the ring after that. The kid admitted that the champ had almost succeeded.

"That baby's got no sense of humor," the kid said. "I got to watch him."

"What did you do besides watch him?" I asked pointedly.

"Nothing yet." The kid had understood the question. He told me he hadn't tried to fight back. He said he'd take it for a while.

"And you know something funny, mister? The champ's scared. Even while he's beating hell out of me, he's scared. I can tell."

That figured.

"Perhaps," I ventured, "it's because he doesn't think you're human."

The kid's grin broadened. He was more relaxed than I'd ever seen him. "That's probably it," he agreed. "And it just goes to show you how far wrong a guy can be. Right, mister?"

"Right."

First chance I got, I told Angelo what the kid was doing. "He's really giving the champ a good time. Maybe that'll teach the big phony not to shoot his mouth off."

Angelo still didn't like it.

"Mr. Evans," he said, "the more I think about it, the more positive I am that you're setting this thing up for Mike and me."

"What makes you think that, Angelo?"

"I'll tell you what, Mr. Evans. It's because the only alternative is that you're setting it up for that headline-happy boss of yours. And I don't want to believe that you'd make suckers of Mike and me just for the sake of a story."

Angelo smiled bleakly and walked off. He'd nicely paid me back in kind. I watched him trounce two rugged and willing sparring partners.

He's about ready to make his move, I thought. *It won't be long.*

It wasn't long.

It was sooner even than I had expected.

Chapter Twenty

"PRETTY FACE LOOKED me up," the kid told me when we met the next morning at the eatery for breakfast. "You figured he would, didn't you, mister?"

"Yes," I said. I'd not only thought he would, I'd gambled he would. And now I was suddenly afraid. I wanted to ask a question and yet I hesitated. Everything hinged on the outcome of that encounter. My plans, Angelo's future, Mike's dream, the kid's salvation (or was the word redemption?); even Borden's standing as an oracle of sorts. Everything.

The kid was grinning. Was it *at* me? Or with me? Had he been playing me for a sucker? Was he just waiting for me to ask so he could sneer in psychopathic triumph and say, "You're a damn fool, mister. A big, stupid, fat, dumb, and happy hoosier. What do you think I am, a square with holes in his head? Sure, he looked me up. I was waiting for him. I wanted the pretty-faced bastard to come to me. Only I got a surprise for you, mister. It didn't turn out like you thought it would. Now you can go visit your pretty hero in the hospital. Yeah, you goddammed right; I sent him back there. I intended to all along. But don't take it so rough, mister. These things happen when you Square Johns start believing those pinheads that write books with happy endings. Well, see you around."

The kid's eyes searched my face. We'd become friends. Or had we? Yes, dammit, we had! I was letting my imagination work overtime. I didn't rate the kid's confidence if I was going to doubt him at the first crucial turn and with no reason whatever for doing so.

"Would you care to tell me about it?" I said as calmly as possible.

"Sure," the kid said. "Why not?"

Their encounter, as related by the kid, had been short, if not sweet; "clean" in its absence of the extraneous, uncluttered. Angelo had been waiting for him when he had left

139

the champ's training quarters and had wasted no time on preliminaries or posturing.

"Listen, friend," Angelo had said, his voice metal-hard, "I don't know what you're up to and I don't care. But let's get one thing straight. I don't need anybody to soften up the guys I'm going to fight."

"So?" the kid had mocked.

"So this!" Angelo had replied. A wicked right, Angelo's Sunday punch, had knocked the kid sprawling, stunned him. Angelo had jerked him back to his feet, told him off.

"And any time you want me, friend, you know where to find me."

That had been it. Without frills.

"Pretty face has got guts; more than I thought," the kid said. "He's got a wallop, too." The kid laughed softly and rubbed his chin. His eyes were thoughtful. "You know, mister, I've been dumped by a bar or a blackjack or when I was ganged, but that's the first time one guy by himself ever knocked me off my feet with one punch." He paused.

I waited.

"Maybe," he added quietly, "it's a sign I can't take it anymore."

Tragically, I thought, perhaps it was—and cold fingers played along my spine. The physical machine could take only so much. It wasn't constructed to be pounded and smashed repeatedly, savagely. The brain especially wasn't designed to absorb the blows, the violent batterings the kid's had. You had only to be present at the post-mortem of a professional fighter who had died of cerebral injuries to have this fact driven home.

The doctors have a saw; it greatly resembles a butcher's saw, and they use it to cut the skull. They work impersonally, efficiently, neither gently nor ungently. Their sawing completed, they lift off the top of the head and remove the brain. They point out the gross damage, the hemorrhaged area, the change in hue generally, the external hardening of the cerebrum, and the many other, more subtle differences. It's a sight you don't forget. You can't. . . .

The kid never told me why he had let Angelo read him off. But I was certain I knew. So I made it a point to be at Larson's Gym that day before Angelo finished his workout and left. We were alone when I spoke to him.

"I hear you settled accounts with the kid."

140

"All right," Angelo said sharply, "you heard. Now what does that make me?" His look was troubled, defensive, almost sullen. There was a tautness about him.

Something was radically wrong.

What?

"A man," I said. "It makes you a man."

"That's a laugh," Angelo said harshly. "And one of these days, *Mr*. Evans, you'll wake up to the fact that the joke's on you."

"I don't get it," I said, puzzled.

"You will," Angelo told me.

He walked away, the psychological monkey still clinging to his back, riding him, bad.

It didn't make sense—then. For a moment anxiety made me almost physically ill. I kept asking myself what possibly could have gone wrong. The question made my head spin and the next thing I knew it wasn't a question at all but a nagging accusation. Somewhere I'd bobbled. Where? A dozen times I went back over the ground and still I found no clue to the answer. It became clear then that I didn't have all the facts. However overworked it was, the analogy of the man trying to work a jigsaw puzzle with some of the pieces missing was apt. Tormentingly so.

Charley Evans, I thought fervently, *don't let your foot slip. Too much is at stake. Remember, this is your one chance to prove the cynics and the wise guys wrong, dead wrong.*

I didn't go straight to the office after my unsettling talk with Angelo. I went to the park, walked for several minutes, then sat on a bench in a deserted spot and fed the pigeons. I looked at the sky, too; at majestic cloud formations piled one atop the other, their white ranks dressed with military precision. Out on the lake a solitary swan swam slowly toward me.

I thought—or at least my mind kept working, almost against my will. It had begun months ago, when Borden had called me into his cluttered cubicle of an office. The dramatis personae had been assembled, had played their assigned roles. In the unfolding events had been a discernible relationship, a unifying element. Now it was about to end. Only the ending was in doubt, the two possible endings: the "happy," poetically right one and the caricatural, mockingly wrong one. Which would it be? I couldn't be sure. It depended, I felt, upon whether hope and faith exerted an influence on

141

such matters. Or determinism and determination. And whether there were in fact as well as in romantic fancy self-executing laws of social justice which could be brought somehow into operation.

A letter from Janey was waiting for me at the office, a friendly, deeply concerned letter. "I'll come," she had written, "the minute you believe I should."

I wanted to tell her to come immediately. But even then it might be too late. Right that instant might be too late. Whatever the risk, I had to stick to my original schedule. I decided I didn't dare ask her to come for at least another week, until the training period was concluded. Otherwise, if he learned, the kid would believe I was dealing from a stacked deck. He'd be convinced I didn't trust him. I said a little prayer.

The waiting was hell.

What followed was worse.

Chapter Twenty-one

DURING THE LAST days of the training period, the kid really worked on the champ. He drove him crazy, taunting him, withering those murderous, two-fisted attacks, grinning at the champ's blind fury. It got so bad that even I couldn't stand to watch the punishment the kid was absorbing.

"For God's sake," I said one day, "don't let that big baboon hurt you!"

"Don't worry, mister," the kid said. "He ain't hurting me." With no trace of self-pity in his voice, the kid added, "I got hurt so bad a long time ago that nobody can ever hurt me again."

Only occasionally during those torrid sessions did the kid open up, just often enough to keep the smart boys predicting that he'd pulverize the champ before he was through. Afterward, the smarties changed their tune. They said the champ was a fox, a sly cookie, that he'd been waiting for the kid to make just one mistake. Then, desperate, in a fear-and-ridicule-born rage, with time running out on him, the champ dared wait no longer. That's the way they told it, and that's almost the way it was. Almost but not quite.

Following an especially furious exchange, the champ made his play. He pointed down to the kid's shoes and mumbled something. The kid grinned, contemptuously dropped his guard and looked down. It was a trick even the rankest amateur knew better than fall for, and the kid was no amateur. The champ packed every ounce of power he possessed into the right hand he threw.

The blow broke the kid's neck. It spun him around. His knees buckled. He collapsed. The grin, they say, never left the kid's fist-smashed face. And the way they tell it, the champ, wild-eyed, stood over the kid and snarled in insane triumph, "I got ya, ya grinning bastard, I got ya!" It wasn't a pretty scene, the way I hear it.

When I received the word, I rammed my old coupé

through traffic and red lights to the hospital. The kid, I was informed bluntly, was dying.

"But there *must* be something you can do!"

There wasn't.

"Is he conscious?"

"Yes."

"Can I see him?"

They told me no at first, but I insisted I had to. I was prepared to bluff, bribe, and argue my way past the whole staff if necessary. Finally the doctor in charge gave me five minutes. "If he lasts that long," the doctor said.

The kid was in agony, his face a twisted mask of pain, but he smiled when I entered. This time the smile wasn't weird; there was real warmth in it. It was human, too.

I stood at the side of the kid's bed, looking down at him. The kid was glad to see me. I could tell. Neither of us said anything for ten or fifteen seconds. It was the kid who spoke first. I had to bend down to hear him.

"That was a good proposition you made me, mister."

The irony was as sharp as a battle-honed sword.

"Dammit," I said, "it didn't include this."

"I'm sorry," the kid apologized. "But . . ."

But!

Sure, I'd known about that "but" all along, but I'd tried to kid myself. This time, I'd thought, the ending would be different, and yet I had realized I was bucking impossible odds. Or really no odds at all.

The kid, with a touch of grim pride, told me in a tortured whisper what had happened. He said he hoped Angelo beat the champ to a pulp. He added that Angelo would make a good champ. "Tell him I said so." Then he hesitated. Finally he whispered, self-consciously:

"Tell me something, mister, and don't give me no con. Do you think maybe after I kick off that I'll see my mother and Maura and that I'll be able to be with them for a little while at least?"

I told him I was sure he would. I believed that. I had to. And I told him, as well, that I was positive his sister Janey would take good care of his small son.

"That's good," the kid said, satisfied. "That's good. And it's best this way, mister."

Then he died.

His body shuddered and he lay still. . . .

I should have made a dash for the nearest phone and reported excitedly to Borden: "The kid's dead." But I didn't. Instead, I just sat there numbly, feeling helpless and even a little angry. I watched as they transferred him to a gurney, pulled a sheet up over his face and wheeled him away. I got up then and stared out the window across the top of the city. An interne who had remained behind said, "You're Charley Evans, the sports columnist, aren't you?"

I looked around and nodded. "Yes."

"I remember that first piece you did on him. Called him a killer, didn't you?"

"Yeah, I called him a killer."

"He must have been a pretty ferocious character."

"I guess he was," I said.

"What makes a guy like that?" the interne asked rhetorically.

"It's a long story."

"Sure," the interne said.

Then I understood why the interne had stayed behind and struck up a conversation. This was the hospital's polite way of asking me to do my brooding somewhere else.

"Be seeing you around," I said.

"Drive slow," the interne told me. He probably was wondering what sort of strange bird I could be to give a damn one way or the other over one tough kid's death.

I found a row of pay phones on the first floor next to the information desk and called Tom Layton.

"Tom," I asked in a hollow voice I hardly recognized as my own, "did you hear the news?"

"I heard the kid was hurt working out with the champ."

"He's dead, Tom."

There was a long pause. When the young psychiatrist had no comment, I added bitterly, "And just before he died he told me that I'd made him a good proposition."

"You don't sound as though you agreed."

"Should I?"

"You gave him what he wanted most: a chance to give his twisted existence some meaning."

"Sure," I grunted sourly. "I'm like the doctor who made his patient die to prove he was sick."

Tom Layton ignored my sarcasm. "And now it's up to you to make people understand about his kind of sickness."

"Tom," I said, "I don't like the price *he* had to pay. Some-

145

how now I don't feel much like a crusader. And what do I tell his sister Janey?"

"The same thing you tell your conscience—the truth."

The line went dead. I was on my own. That was the way it had to be. I either succeeded in following through without a crutch or I folded up and admitted the job was too big for me.

I called the agency for the air lines and got the information I needed. Then I dialed the operator and asked for long distance. It took fifteen minutes to get the call through but only five to say what had to be said. When I hung up, I remembered Borden. I got this editorial cacodemon on the line and filled him in.

"The champ's right hand broke the kid's neck. The kid's dead."

The silence that followed didn't indicate either sympathy or distress on Borden's part. He was consulting his watch. "We still got plenty of time to make the sports final."

"Yeah," I growled back, "the kid timed the whole thing so that it wouldn't inconvenience you. Thoughtful of him, wasn't it?"

"You'll feel better tomorrow," Borden said, ready to dismiss my personal reaction as wholly irrelevant, if not presumptuous. He might as well have said I was only a story machine, not a feeling person. "Now how soon'll you have a feature ready for me?" The impatience had crept back into his voice.

"When I feel better," I said.

"Hey . . . !"

The click of the connection being broken was a sound Borden understood. *Hey, hell,* I thought.

I took another long walk in the park. This time I had all the pieces to the puzzle, all the answers to the questions which had given me so many sleepless nights. My problem now was ingesting and accepting them. *De mortuis nil nisi bonum* needed to be reversed. I intended to speak angrily of the living for the dead. I owed the kid and myself that much.

What makes a guy like that?

Wasn't it pain and terror and not being wanted? Wasn't it picking the wrong parent or parents, too, and the workings of chance in a hundred different ways? Wasn't it being a child of hate, finally, an emotional orphan whose sneering coldness was an urgent defense, an implied admission of being otherwise vulnerable, that became in time a condi-

146

tioned reflex? Didn't guile and cynicism help man the walls of this bastion only because more honorable guardians had fled, leaving a menaced entity undefended? And wasn't fear, in the beginning, the tyrannical master which sought always to degrade, and made of existence a special kind of hell?

Look and you would always find the Authority figure who had precipitated the crisis from which the psychopathic personality was formed. And often, however successful their social adjustment, these authoritarians with their little dictator complexes were as psychologically sick and as spiritually impoverished as such "killers" as the kid. Would the day ever come when we would frankly recognize this fact? Or was our culture too hopelessly shot through with cops and robbers, good guys and bad guys thinking? I thought not. In time we would substitute vision for vengeance. We would rise above our own fears and insecurity and senseless prejudices, and when we did we would build a better world, one whose architect was neither force nor violence, retribution nor suspicion. The alternative was increasing barbarism, the propagation of doubt, the loss of freedom and, ultimately, a nuclear Armageddon.

The kid was dead. A psychopath was dead. At last that psychological death sentence had been carried out—and the kid thought I had done him a favor. But he would have hated my guts if he'd thought I had any idea of apologizing for him. I didn't. Giving a spiritual execution meaning, making people grasp its implications for them, wasn't to seek to justify or excuse. It simply answered the question an interne had asked off-handedly: "What makes a guy like that?"

What makes him unable to show "weakness" and unwilling to trust altogether any other human being?

Knowing the answers, having all the pieces to the puzzle, made me feel much older than my fifty-odd years, for now it was my responsibility to reduce those answers to words and to help people see not only the kind of person the kid had become but the sort of individual he might have been.

I turned back toward where I had left my coupé parked.

Chapter Twenty-two

JANEY FLEW in the next morning, accompanied by the elderly, self-effacing pastor who had befriended Maura. I met them at the airport. An early morning overcast hid the sun. The day was gray.

"I'm Evans," I told them. "Charley Evans." Right then I wasn't particularly proud of the fact.

"It was very kind of you to meet us," the pastor said.

Janey smiled her agreement. Our eyes met.

Kind? I thought. *Kind!* They meant it, too. *Sure,* I told myself bitterly, *it's very kind of me. And it was very kind of me to help put the kid in his grave.*

My eyes dropped to their bags. "Here," I said quickly, trying to hide my embarrassment, my confusion, "let me help you with those." I went on: "My car's right over there. I'll show you."

They followed with no word of reproach when I lengthened my stride. I would have liked to run, not so much away from them as from myself.

On the way to the city, the pastor coughed softly to get my attention. I guess I'd drawn rather far into my shell, for he had to cough twice more before I realized they had something to say to me, a request to make.

"I'm sorry," I said.

"We understand," he told me sympathetically.

Then Janey spoke, for the first time. "We were wondering if you would take us to see him."

"Now?" I asked, not able to conceal my surprise altogether. "I mean before you're settled?"

"Yes," she said. "Please. If it won't inconvenience you too greatly."

"Not at all," I assured her.

She added, "It has been a long time."

"A long time," I repeated, nodding. "You know the

unusual circumstances under which he died?" I said awkwardly.

"Yes."

"Well, it seems now the coroner's office is holding his body. Just a formality, of course, until the matter's straightened up."

"But that doesn't mean we can't see him, does it?"

"No," I conceded. "Only—"

Only the kid might not then be a pretty sight, I wanted to say.

"I understand," Janey said. "You want to spare us. But it will be all right. You see, it's just that we feel he may be waiting for us. We want him to know that we're here."

I phoned ahead and made the arrangements. His body had gone to the morgue. By the time we arrived, they had pulled him from the icebox and laid him out on one of the slabs. A sheet had been thrown over him, leaving the face and the feet exposed. They had the peculiar gray pallor of death about them. The eyes were closed. A tag was tied to the great right toe.

Smiling slightly, sadly, Janey said, "Hello, Buddy."

The elderly pastor bowed his white head, closed his eyes, and prayed in a low, firm voice for the repose of the kid's soul. Completing the prayer, this kindly old man of the cloth turned to me. "I am certain," he said, "that the boy has found a peace he never knew in this life."

"With Maura and his mother," I added.

The pastor nodded. "And with God, who uses us on occasion in strange ways."

"I'm glad you were with him when he died," Janey said, meaning it.

"And you understand why I didn't send for you sooner?"

"Yes, perfectly."

The three of us had a long talk. I had never met two finer people. They convinced me I wasn't a cynical newspaper guy who would do anything for a story, after all.

At the hotel Janey said with conviction, "You did the right thing." The kindly old pastor's head bobbed in agreement.

"Thanks," I said. "Believe me, those words mean a lot. Now if you'll pardon me for a few hours, I'll do my part in seeing that his death wasn't in vain."

And only then, with Borden on the verge of a nervous

breakdown over my delay, did I tell the world about the kid
—not the psychopathic killer, but the boy who got lost in
a jungle. My bitter, angry story about him, front-paged,
ran for three successive days. It was given national coverage. Readers across the country were shocked, outraged.
Letters began to pour in. Sportscasters, commentators, and
columnists lambasted the champ for pulling the stunt he had,
with Borden, in full cry, leading the editorial attack.

A coroner's inquest was held. The D.A.'s office was con-
ducting an investigation. There was talk that a manslaughter
charge would be filed. The title fight was rumored off. Then
it was postponed a week.

On the day my concluding article about the kid appeared,
with the fight only four days off, I received a frantic tele-
phone call from Mike. Angelo had broken training and
disappeared! Hours later we found him, alone and bleary-
eyed drunk, in the back booth of a skid-row bar.

"Go 'way," he told us.

"What's wrong, son?" Mike asked.

"Go 'way," Angelo repeated, waving vaguely. "Go 'way
and lemme 'lone. Don't wanta talk. Don't even wanta think.
Jus' wanta get so damn' drunk I can't remember who I am."

It took us almost an hour to learn what was tearing him
to pieces. "All right," he finally said, grimacing. "You gotta
know. I'll tell you."

Angelo had hit the kid with brass knuckles!

The incredible irony of those brass knucks I kept to
myself, but Angelo was a perceptive youngster. He knew.
Indirectly my series on the kid had told him. Unwittingly
I'd been the one to indict him. He didn't realize that I
hadn't known about the missing piece of the puzzle involving
him. So his actions and reactions, ironically, had proved him
right: the joke was on me, yet not in the bitter way he
thought. In another way.

"Maybe it's a sign I can't take it any more," the kid had
said.

Now the question was—could the rest of us take it?

We drove Angelo to my place and sobered him up,
talked to him. Then I made a phone call. "Get over here just
as fast as you can," I concluded.

Angelo had hated the kid; now he hated himself, and hate
was like a cancer. It would destroy him just as it had destroyed the kid unless excised swiftly and utterly. And this
wasn't a job for a newspaperman or a psychiatrist. It was

150

a job for a woman, a certain woman, young, slim, dark-haired, possessed of a beauty that was warmly feminine. A woman who had known tragedy in her earlier years but who, rather than becoming embittered or hardened, had won from those dark years a quiet courage and a compassionate strength. A woman who had not yet married but who would make a splendid wife.

After a few minutes there was a knock at the door.

"Come in," I called out.

A young woman with all these qualifications entered.

"Angelo," I said, "I want you to meet Janey, the kid's sister. I want you to listen with both ears to what she has to tell you."

"Hello, Angelo," Janey said softly, smiling.

Angelo looked up. He managed a smile. "Janey," he said, "the beautiful angel come to minister to one of the foolish and fallen." He continued, "You know, they call me Angel, too. Isn't that ridiculous?"

"No, Angelo," Janey said, "I don't think it's ridiculous at all."

"You don't?" Angelo said bitterly. "Then you mustn't know the whole story."

"Rather," Janey said, "I believe it is you, Angelo, who doesn't know the whole story."

We left them alone.

But "The Rag" didn't. It had learned about Angelo's disappearance, about his getting drunk, and had wasted no time in headlining his actions and furnishing its readers with a vicious interpretation of them. That yellow sheet's version boiled down to this: with the kid dead, Angelo was scared silly. It was even suggested that he'd had a hand in planting the kid on the champ, "with the connivance of a certain local newspaper and for reasons that will hardly tax the imagination of the reader. But," continued the muscular piece, fairly exuding virtue, "this Machiavellian scheme has backfired on the principals."

The kid's death was righteously dismissed with a flick of the editorial hand. The writer wrote the "accident" off "as a case of a brutal psychopath getting exactly what he had asked for. Intelligent sports fans won't be fooled by all the caterwauling." Having thus "put the situation in its proper perspective," "The Rag" fired its final big gun: "We predict, without hesitation, that the would-be challenger either will beg off meeting the champion or, if forced to go through

151

with the fight, that he will be exposed as the sorriest pretender to lay claim to a boxing title to come along in a decade. He won't last three rounds."

Borden was smoking. "We'll sue those idiots for libel!" he bellowed. "We'll make 'em eat that damned drivel!" Then he shifted his ground and his battered green eyeshade. "But what if it's true?" he muttered, scowling. He fixed me with his best district attorney's stare. "Evans," he shouted, "you've got your fine Italian hand in this business up to your shoulder blade and I'm not sure I like it. If you've walked me into a trap, I'll roast you. I'll make you sorry you were born!"

"You through with your third degree?" I asked, fighting to control my temper.

"Not quite," Borden retorted. "I've got a question and I want an honest, yes-or-no answer. Has Marino lost his guts or hasn't he?"

"No," I said angrily, "he hasn't. But now I'm beginning to think you have. Otherwise you'd be listening to what I have to tell you instead of running off at the mouth like you are."

To his credit, Borden listened.

We buried the kid the morning of the title fight, and later, with the kindly old pastor's assistance, we arranged to have Maura's remains placed beside his.

Angelo had insisted on paying all the expenses and, with Janey's help, attending personally to the details. He ignored what "The Rag" had said, what it was saying. He was trying to make amends.

At the graveside, I told him, "You can do that tonight, Angelo. The kid expected you to win. He told me you'd make a good champ and I agreed with him."

Janey put her hand in Angelo's. "I agree with my brother, too," she said. "You'll win. I'm sure of it."

"What I've got to win," Angelo told us grimly, but without dramatics, "is more than the title."

He was right.

Back at the office Borden was waiting for me. "Come into my office, Charley. There's something I want to show you."

"Something" was a copy of a newspaper, roughed out

152

emblazoned EXTRA, and headlined: MARINO WINS LIGHT HEAVY TITLE BY KO.

I experienced a sudden feeling of warmth for this cocky banty rooster of a boss. "You've been looking into that crystal ball again, General."

"No," Borden said, shaking his bald head from side to side. "I've been listening to you. Remember?"

"Sure. But I also remember that in this day of TV and other electronic communication marvels they don't put out extras past edition time anymore."

Borden shrugged elaborately. "Maybe 'they' don't. I'm going to. The publisher's given me the green light. And I've got it all worked out: we'll have our extra on the streets within ninety minutes after the fight's over."

"In that case," I said casually, "I guess that leaves only one trivial question."

"Yeah," Borden said impatiently, "what's that?"

"What happens if Angelo loses?"

Borden gagged.

"We," he said ominously, "don't talk about that."

The train was an hour late but I stuck out the waiting with Janey and the pastor. And from the first moment that I set eyes on the little old lady and the sleeping toddler she carried I was glad I had.

"There they are!" Janey said and ran forward to meet them. The pastor and I followed. "Martha's going to miss the little one. As you know, she's helped Janey raise him from the day Janey brought him home and I'm afraid the little fellow's stolen our hearts."

"But when Janey asked your wife to bring the boy it only was so that all four of you could be together and return home together," I protested.

"That's true," the pastor said. "Yet while I'm an old man, Mr. Evans, I like to believe that I'm not entirely a blind one. In short"—this kind old pastor's smile was both tender and sad—"I'm of the opinion that Martha and I will be returning home alone."

I didn't try to pretend I didn't know what he was talking about. I did.

Then we were within earshot of the embracing women. Janey took the little guy, kissed him, and then introduced me to the pastor's tiny wife. She was as warm and real a

153

person as Janey and the pastor. Just meeting her was a pleasure.

"So this is the writing man," she said, offering me her hand. "God bless you. God bless you for the kindness you showed him"—the kid—"before his death and for the sensible things you have written about him after it."

I thanked her and meant every word.

The little guy had awakened. His eyes were on me. After a mighty yawn, he said, dropping the *r* in the second word, "Hi, writing man." But it was the smile on that very young face that won me over completely. Here was the dream for the future that the kid and Maura had shared; in one sense, here they were. Here was their flesh and their blood, their love. This smiling, golden-haired little boy was what they had left to us in trust.

"Would you care to hold him?" Janey asked.

"Of course he would," smiled the pastor's tiny wife.

Janey passed him to me and he threw his chubby arms around my neck. On the way to the car I'd borrowed—my coupé wouldn't hold us all—he told me all about his exciting ride on the choo-choo. From the outset we got along famously.

When we arrived at Angelo's apartment he'd just awakened. Before the funeral that morning he'd weighed in; after it, Mike had brought him here to relax by taking a nap. I'd told him and Mike I'd be around sometime before they left for the stadium. "Got a little surprise on tap for you two characters," I'd said.

Now Angelo was down on one knee, offering a hand to the suddenly solemn, wide-eyed little boy who stood in front of him. Almost shyly, at his Aunt Janey's urging, the kid's small son took a step forward and acknowledged this handsome, smiling stranger by extending his own right hand for a man-to-man greeting. Then, hopefully, he asked a little boy's desperate question:

"Are you my daddy?"

The question caught all of us off guard. It was Angelo who recovered first and relieved the tension. He shook his head. "No, little man, I'm sorry to say I'm not. But I knew your daddy well before he had to go away on a long trip."

"Why'd he go?"

"Mostly on your account and also because he wanted to see your mother."

154

"She's in heaven. God came and took her there and left me with Aunty Jane."

Angelo nodded. "Yes, I know. And now do you think we can be good friends? I'd like that."

The little guy frowned briefly while considering this friendly stranger's offer. Then his head bobbed happily up and down and that infectious smile lit his face. They could be friends. It was like a jury's verdict of "Not guilty" in a death penalty case.

We had to go.

The elderly pastor and his wife would take care of the little guy while Janey and I and the others were at the fight. The zero hour was very close at hand.

Chapter Twenty-three

HERE IT WAS, the Big Night, the payoff.

Some forty thousand screaming fans had jammed our out-door stadium. Reporters from all the major papers and wire services around the country were at ringside. The champ and Angelo both had just entered the ring. Flash bulbs exploded as their gloves were laced on. You could feel the tension. It was a hot, sticky night, made worse by the brilliant blue-white TV lights which burned down like smokeless blow torches. Angelo was an overwhelming sentimental favorite, but the smart money favored the champ seven to three.

"Your attention, ple-e-e-z!" bawled the announcer.

"Fifteen rounds for the light heavyweight championship of the world," he continued with weighty importance. Then he introduced, "at one hundred seventy-three pounds, the popular challenger"—he paused briefly and dramatically stabbed his right index finger in Angelo's direction—"Angelo MAH-REE-NO!"

The partisan crowd shouted its lungs out. In the opposite corner the champ glared balefully at the smiling, handsome challenger. He acknowledged his own introduction—and the swelling roar of boos, screamed insults, and catcalls that followed it—by glowering at the crowd.

The referee motioned both fighters to the center of the ring. "You men know the rules of the State Athletic Commission. This being a championship fight, the mandatory eight count and the three-knockdowns-in-one-round rule requiring termination of the fight have been waived. The man scoring the knockdown will go to the farthest neutral corner and wait there until I signal him to resume fighting. Break when I tell you but protect yourselves at all times. I want a clean fight. Shake hands now and come out fighting. Good luck to you both."

Angelo and the champ touched gloves, returned to their respective corners. The crowd quieted, waiting, expectant. The bell clanged, sounding loud in the silence. I drew a deep breath. This was the moment Mike had waited thirty long years for.

Angelo did a baffling thing. He didn't come out fighting. Instead, he walked flat-footed toward the champ with his guard down, smiling in a strange, fixed way. Surprised, suspecting a trick of some kind, the champ warily circled his man. He jabbed cautiously, twice. He hooked. Then he uncorked a sudden, looping right hand. It caught Angelo on the chin, decked him.

The crowd gasped at the suddenness of what had happened. Borden, seated on my left between me and Tom Layton, screamed hoarsely. Janey, on my right, said, anguished, "Oh, no! No!" I flinched.

What was wrong?

Angelo got up, was pounded into the ropes, decked again. The mocking smile hadn't left his face, wouldn't. He made it to his feet at seven, faced the champ contemptuously. The champ, always a brutal opportunist, closed in for the kill. A barrage of blows drove Angelo across the ring. Still Angelo was making no real effort to defend himself. The champ unloosed his heaviest artillery. In the stunned, oppressive silence, you could hear the sound of each blow. Angelo took an inhuman beating; finally, with two minutes of the round gone, he sagged slowly to the canvas. A groan went up. Everyone thought it was over.

It can't be! I thought desperately.

Angelo had fallen just above us. He saw me and squinted quizzically. I registered through the soup-thick fog in his mind. His mocking, now lopsided grin broadened. He struggled to his feet, barely beating the count. The referee looked at him sharply when he wiped his gloves.

"I'm okay," Angelo insisted.

"Then fight," the referee said.

"I am—in my own way."

Angelo lasted out the round on raw courage alone, repeatedly taking the champ's best punches. They would have torn an ordinary man in two. It was awful to watch. He was down twice more before the bell sounded. Like a drunken man, he staggered to his corner. There, baffled and frantic, Mike met him. Mike talked, fretted and pleaded while Angelo, his dark eyes focused on the cocky, hairy-bodied champ, listened and smiled eerily, saying nothing.

In a tizzy, Borden turned on me and shouted, "What's the

157

matter with that Marino, is he crazy? He's getting murdered and he tells the referee he's fighting!"

In a calm voice Dr. Tom Layton told Borden, answering for me, "Angelo knows what he's doing. In fact, you might say that he's following my advice."

"What!" Borden bellowed. "I might've known it!" He slapped his palm against his forehead. "I should've known this is the kind of advice a headshrinker would give."

Carried away with himself, Borden cupped his hands to his mouth, megaphone-fashion, and let go a mighty blast. "Forget what the headshrinker told you, Marino, and fight! Do you hear me—FIGHT!"

Suddenly it dawned on me what Angelo was doing and why. I should have known from the first.

Of course—he was remembering the kid, paying him a magnificent tribute, making amends the hard way, in a daring, unbelievably courageous way. He was proving to himself and the kid and "The Rag" and the world that he could take it. He was leaving absolutely no doubt. Clearly, possibly suicidally, he intended to win the title the way the kid would have wanted him to or he wouldn't win it at all!

The blood pounded in my ears; I felt a prickly sensation at the back of my neck. I leaned across an agitated Borden and said excitedly to Tom Layton, "Then Angelo came to see you after he disappeared on us."

Tom Layton nodded. "Just yesterday, as a matter of fact. I suspected the trouble and invited him over."

"And he told you about using the——"

"—brass knuckles? Yes. He did."

"Say," Borden demanded, practically frothing at the mouth, "what're you two eggheads mumbling about, anyway?"

"You're supposed to be the master mind," I shot back. "You should know." I was in no mood for his antics.

The little man quivered with indignation, frustration. He leaped to his feet. He put on quite a show. "Evans," he shouted, "you're fired!"

Obviously unimpressed with Borden's theatrics, a big guy behind us tapped my vibrating ex-boss on the shoulder and said, "Down in front."

I didn't say anything. The temptation was strong to muzzle the little egomaniac, to bark at him, "For just once in your self-centered life, get smart to yourself. Try to grasp the courageous thing that boy in the ring is doing." But I knew it was useless. So I kept my mouth shut.

The bell rang.

The second round was a brutal, sickening repetition of the first. Somehow Angelo survived it (though Borden almost didn't). The beating Angelo took and the noises Borden made were indescribable.

Mike was on the verge of collapse when the round ended and Angelo, virtually out on his feet, headed for the wrong corner. The crowd was stunned. There were isolated cries of "Stop it! Stop it!"

Mike wanted to throw in the towel but the Angel shook his head in violent protest. His lips formed one word: "No!" The boxing commission's doctor entered the ring to examine him. I held my breath and sent up a silent prayer. Janey's fingers dug into my forearm.

"I'm all right," Angelo said. "I know what I'm doing."

"But he's not fighting," the referee complained to the doctor.

"I'm ready to begin," Angelo said. He was still smiling; it wasn't a pretty smile.

The doctor hesitated, undecided. Everything hinged on his decision.

Borden in his distress may have saved the day. He forever after would believe that he had. "Hell," he boomed in a voice that could be heard in the next county, "anybody ought to be able to see that Marino isn't hurt. That boy's tough; he can take it! If anybody needs protection, it's the champ. The big bum's shot his bolt. And if this fight's stopped it'll be because somebody's put the fix in."

The crowd, electrified, roared its wholehearted assent. Doubt and fear had vanished. Angelo was this crowd's boy, its champion.

The boxing commission's doctor turned an angry red in the face. "Marino's physically able to continue," he snapped.

"I'll give you another round," the referee said. "But you'd better start fighting or I'm stopping it and that's final."

The ten-second warning buzzer sounded.

"I guess I told 'em!" Borden crowed.

"Down in front, baldy," the big guy behind us said.

Angelo was off his stool and on his feet. He was looking over and down at us. He winked and I wiped the cold perspiration from my forehead. I sensed he'd won his crazy, magnificant gamble. My pulse quickened. "It's going to be all right now," I assured Janey.

She smiled. "I do hope so."

159

In the third Angelo came to life. While his fogged mind cleared, while the glaze left his eyes, his educated left hand repeatedly stabbed the champ off balance. The champ's bull-like rushes weren't as effective; his deadliest punches were smothered or went wild. He'd lost his bully's swaggering, arrogant confidence. Things were no longer going all his way. Toward the end of the round a sizzling left hook rocked him, forced him to clinch. The crowd came to its feet with a roar.

The tide was turning!

From that moment, late in the third round, Angelo took command of the fight. He coolly met the champ's desperate lunges. He calmly gave the champ an unforgettable boxing lesson. In the seventh he unhesitatingly accepted the champ's growled invitation to slug it out. For fully half a minute they stood toe to toe and savagely bombed each other with their heaviest guns. It was the champ who dropped. He was up at the count of two, a madman now that he saw defeat closing in on him. Relentlessly, Angelo smashed him to the canvas three more times in the round before he remained sprawled there, helpless. Up and down went the referee's right arm.

". . . seven . . . eight . . . nine . . ."

Ten!

It was all over! "The winner and new light heavyweight champion of the world!" shouted the announcer into the P.A. system. "Angelo MAH-REE-NO!" The time: two minutes and forty-nine seconds of the seventh round. The crowd went mad. The place was bedlam. Enthusiasts stormed the ring.

Mike was wildly, unashamedly embracing his boy, tears of joy streaming down his leathery cheeks. Angelo waved to Janey, grinning, happy, the grim, avenging look gone from his battered face. Borden had jumped up on his seat and was triumphantly pounding Tom Layton on the back, roaring, "We did it! We did it! Our boy came through!" Then his voice cracked; it died with a high-pitched squeak. Like that day at the office, his mouth continued to work furiously but not a sound came out of it, not even a "glob, glob."

"Oh, oh, I've been expecting that," Tom Layton said wryly, shouting to make himself heard. "Mr. Borden," he counseled, "relax. You've literally shouted and screamed yourself voice-less"—a result I regarded as at least twenty years overdue. Talk about poetic justice!

"It's only a temporary condition," the doctor added consolingly.

"Too bad," I said.

Here, I thought, *is where I have some fun.* I turned to Janey, took her arm. "Angelo's expecting you," I said. "Let's beat the crowd to his dressing room."

I'd shouted loud enough for Borden to hear me. He made a wild, arm-waving, frantic leap from his seat and barricaded our path.

"Down in front, baldy," I said, poker-faced, mimicking the big guy who had sat behind us.

Borden gesticulated frantically; he grew popeyed and purple-faced trying to talk. It appeared as though he might strangle himself with the effort.

I cupped a hand to my ear like an old codger who is hard of hearing. "Eh? What's that? Can't catch a word you're saying."

Again Borden went into his act.

"This character," I said, "either belongs in burlesque or he needs a psychiatrist."

Tom Layton took his cue. "He does appear to be acutely distressed," he observed dryly. "Fortunately I happen to be able to read lips, so perhaps I can help." The doctor asked Borden what was bothering him.

I didn't have to be told what had my larynx-locked ex-boss in a lather—his precious extra.

"Somebody," I said, "remind this pocket-sized troll that he fired me."

Think nothing of it, I was told through Tom Layton. A misunderstanding, I was assured. Mr. Borden wanted me to know he would be happy to rehire me. His eyes laughing, Tom Layton appended, "with a substantial bonus and raise in pay, of course."

"Of course," I said, knowing my doctor friend had ad-libbed that last. I had to fight to keep a straight face. This was getting better all the time. "And of course," I added, "he's also determined to hire you, doctor, as a special consultant."

Janey, anxious to talk to Angelo, excused herself. The crowd swirled past us. The din began to subside.

And Borden almost had a stroke. Or two strokes. Without a doubt the Fates had conspired against him, had put him at the mercy of a headshrinker who could read lips and an eccentric columnist and feature writer who had the temerity to think for himself; and he couldn't even bellow his outrage at such an incomprehensible injustice.

It was too much! Here he had sacrificed his noblest weapon, his voice, to overcome the romantic blunderings of the egg-headed pair and avert final disaster for Angelo—and *this* was to be his reward, capitulation. For in his extremity, Borden direly needed us, needed my yet unwritten words and Tom Layton's voice.

Or no extra.

No triumphant "last" laugh at "The Rag."

Before bowing ungracefully to the inevitable, Borden looked heavenward. In that look was a mute appeal for strength and mild reproach. Then he grinned a seasick grin and offered his hand.

We solemnly shook hands. I again was numbered among the gainfully employed—"with a substantial bonus and raise in pay, of course."

Then Borden went through the ritual of shaking hands with Tom Layton, psychiatrist, and now "special consultant" to a temporarily voiceless sports editor.

"Tom," I said, slapping Borden affectionately on the back (I sternly resisted the temptation to pat him on his bald dome), "do you know the one quality I admire most in this remarkable little boss of mine?"

"What's that?"

"His rare, Rabelaisian sense of humor. Nobody's can come close to comparing with it."

The fantastic part was that Borden took me seriously. He lost the greenish, seasick look and beamed at us. His look seemed to be saying that we might be a couple of picaresque characters but at least we had the good sense to appreciate his finer qualities. Perhaps we weren't hopelessly lost souls after all!

Yes, there it was—a fitting and whimsical footnote to both triumph and tragedy, counterpoint to the grim malady of the soul that had driven the kid to the grave. A tour de force of social myopia. The General Borden syndrome. . . .

Less than two hours later newsboys were hawking our extra with Borden's exultant headline: MARINO WINS LIGHT HEAVY TITLE BY KO.

162

Chapter Twenty-four

IT WAS CLOSE to midnight when Tom Layton, Borden (with a stack of extras under his arm), and I arrived at the Castlemont where Angel's stunning victory was being lavishly and noisily celebrated. It seemed to me the whole city was packed into the big ball room. Somebody spotted us as we entered and shouted, "Speech! Speech!" Everyone present picked up the chant. It boomed from one end of the hall to the other.

"You won't need me," I said and ducked. I'd had enough of the limelight.

With musical fanfare, the mayor convoyed a strutting Borden and Tom Layton to the bandstand and made what I was told was his fifth speech of the evening. No one seemed to mind.

"I now give you," said the speechmaking mayor portentously, with a wave of his pudgy arms, "two of our fair city's foremost citizens and two men who need no introduction." Three minutes later the two men who needed no introduction finally got introduced.

My young psychiatrist friend, never in better form, handled the situation with just the right touch, deftly patting Borden on the ego and next explaining about his temporary vocal infirmity. With his audience in attentive and good-humored custody, Tom then read, with the little man's beaming approval, the "editorial" Borden had written for his extra. After giving "The Rag" its punitive lumps in a surprisingly mild and this-hurts-me-more-than-it-does-you fashion, and making only (for its author) modest mention of the fact that he'd prepared his extra well in advance of the title match, Borden had ended by paying an emotional tribute to a lovable old warrior and our city's courageous new champ.

"They're a great pair! We're proud of them!"

The audience shouted, stamped, and whistled its whole-hearted approval. Borden, his grin extending from ear to ear, took his bow, had his hand pumped by the mayor, and then began to pass out copies of his extra. The orchestra struck up "Hail, Hail, the Gang's All Here." Even I found myself joining in the singing.

Later I worked my way around to Angelo and Janey, who, after a giddy two hours, had retreated to a relatively quiet corner by themselves. I decided I wouldn't be intruding by talking to them for a couple of minutes.

"Hi!" they said in unison, warmly.

I smiled at them. "Congratulations, champ!"

"Gee, Mr. Evans, thanks."

It was obvious that Angelo already had forgotten the terrible beating he had taken. His handsome face was bruised and puffed, one eye was almost closed, his lower lip was sutured, but he was healed and whole inside, where, as Mike had said, it counted most. He'd won—more than the title. He was his own man again, and I was glad, glad because this was the way it should be.

"We owe you a lot, Mr. Evans," Angelo said earnestly. "All of us. More than we'll ever be able to repay. It took tonight to make me realize that."

"Forget it," I said. Sure, I felt good inside, but talk like this made me uneasy, self-conscious. Besides, I didn't think I deserved any credit for doing what I'd done. Rather, and this wasn't any false or phony humility, I felt I should be abidingly grateful for having had the opportunity to demonstrate conclusively that spiritually sick people like the kid's old man were wrong, dead wrong. A sneer or a snarl wasn't the answer. I knew that now, and I knew why. I had the answers. They weren't the glib or clever ones I might have thought at one time.

"No," Janey said, "we won't forget it. We couldn't, not after all you've done and especially not knowing you were the best friend my brother ever had." Janey hesitated, remembering. Then she asked, "You don't think it's wrong for me to be here so soon after Buddy's death?"

"It's really my fault, Mr. Evans," Angelo put in quickly. "I talked her into coming."

"No," I assured them, "it's not wrong. It's right. And it's what he would have wanted. In my opinion, you both owe it to him not to brood over his death or the past but to think about the future."

Angelo was clearly relieved. "Mr. Evans," he said suddenly, "I love Janey!"

Before either Janey or I could say anything, he added

defensively, the words tumbling out: "And nobody can tell me I haven't known her long enough to be sure because I am sure. I'm positive."

Janey blushed; her beautiful young face was radiant.

"Oh," I said, trying to sound like the wise old owl I wasn't.

"I want her to marry me."

"That sounds reasonable enough," I said, nodding at my own sagacity. "Have you asked her yet?"

"Well . . . no," Angelo had to admit. "Not exactly, at least. What I mean is, I was just trying to work up my nerve when you came over."

I laughed. "Angelo, my young friend, I'm afraid this is one time an old bachelor can't help you. But there's a balcony over there"—I pointed—"and a big pumpkin of a moon in the sky. I suggest you ask Janey to accompany you out there for a look at that moon. And after you've both had a good long look, you might ask your question. I've heard that results are usually favorable under such conditions."

Grinning boyishly, Angelo thanked me.

We said our good-bys. I watched them go, arm in arm. "Romantic old fool!" I muttered to myself and swallowed the lump in my throat.

I found Mike by the punch bowl. He looked a lot like the devil-may-care Roughhouse Mike McGuire of thirty years before. Surrounded by an admiring group of sweet young things, he was jokingly telling them what a ferocious character he had been in his youth. He could talk about that now—now that he had a champ. He caught my eye.

"Oh, oh," he said with mock concern, "I better watch what I say now. Here's Charley Evans."

I grinned, but the grin didn't fool him. We had known each other too many years. He led me aside.

"I know how you feel, Charley. I mean about the kid. I think in time I could have learned to like him as much as you did. And believe me, I know if it hadn't been for him, Angelo would never have got to be champ." Mike paused, then added gruffly, "It's a damn shame he had to fall for the oldest gag in the world."

I wanted to tell Mike then but I didn't. I never told anyone except the D.A. and Tom Layton. The kid hadn't fallen for that gag about the busted shoelace. He had deliberately got in the way of the blow that killed him.

That was the reason I spent the rest of the night around the punch bowl, trying to forget. I never quite did.

Conclusion

Wherever and whenever fighters and those who love the fight game gather they speak in awe of a grinning, iron-fisted kid who has become one of the legendary figures of their bruising world. They will tell you proudly how he was the "toughest, craziest sonofabitch" ever to be in the business and this is the highest compliment they can pay a dead gladiator. Arch your eyebrows skeptically, mutter disparagingly, "Oh, I dunno"—and be prepared to fight. Or run like hell while you're still in one piece.

Fighters and the fight crowd may not be, on the whole, the most intellectually sophisticated group extant, and admittedly among it is a vicious, unsavory element, but there isn't a man comprising that group who, because he has been brutally made aware of its value, does not admire openly and honestly that quality which brought us from the trees and keeps us marching toward new horizons—physical courage, guts, if you please, in the face of overwhelming odds. (The impossible odds, of course, in the kid's case were imposed by a fatal affliction of the soul. Unaware of the subtleties implied by a diagnostic label, one old pug put it this way: "That baby just didn't give a damn. Hell, he'd of fought a whole bunch of grizzly bears with his bare hands if the damned bears so much as growled at him.")

The professional fighter's life is not an easy one; it's glamorous only from a distance. Close up it's a rugged, savage, often dog-eat-dog business. Discounting TV's overrated powder puff dandies and ersatz "millers," only a charmed few are born with the natural physical endowments, the temperament and the luck, not to mention the connections, to get to the top, and even champions can be lonely men to whom their hour of fame is, then or later, a mocking curse.

So it is not surprising that fighters and the fight crowd to employ the psychologist's term, have identified with the kid, for legend has it that he was a man even the devil him·

self couldn't bluff or scare—or KO on the square. They tell, rightly, how he came from the slums and how the shattering experiences in his childhood, the violence, the brutality, the clashes with authority, made him the man he was, a guy who defied the malignant gods and who walked alone. "Sure he did some time in the pen," they say. "What about it? Didn't he also sign up to fight over in Korea when a lot of squares were thinkin' up all kinds of reasons why they oughtta be allowed to stay behind? Didn't he stop enough lead to kill ten guys? Didn't the Chinks do their damnedest to break him when they had him in the POW camp?"

No, to them he isn't a hero as the rest of us understand that word. Rather, he's a symbol. In a machine age jungle, where entity, the individuality of the underdog, is ever under attack, the kid retained his. True, in the end, the gods destroyed him, they made him destroy himself, but they were never able to make him cry out for mercy. In a terrible way, he was without fear. Thus, by "normal" standards, he was less than human—and more. And this explains why, as the legend surrounding him grows, he has become nine feet tall.

In an age so fear-ridden, so full of doubt that it can feel secure only by creating awesome weapons too destructively stupefying to imagine, it is no surprise that such an age would create an equally awesome "psychopathic" personality whose attributes should appear, as well as clinically tragic to a few of us, symbolically desirable to many of us. Tragedy and desirability are merely opposite sides of the same coin. It is with this coin that we buy our destinies.

And so the kid lives on in the minds of other men, and this surely is one of the strangest decrees ever to be entered in the statute book of fate. . . .

The kid lives on, too, in another way—through his little guy. In their only meeting, shortly afer the child's birth and Maura's senseless death, the kid had whispered these notable words to his tiny son: "I'll get even for both of us. It'll be up to you to get ahead." The kid fulfilled his part of the pact, and now I am convinced that a happy, growing little boy will fulfill his, too.

The little guy lives here in our city with Angelo and Janey, who were married by the elderly pastor before he and his wife returned home. Janey is expecting a child of her own before long and Angelo has another defense of his title coming up. After this next fight, Angelo plans to retire. He and Mike are going into the sportsgear manufacturing business.

With me it's business at the same old stand—or I should say at the same old Underwood. And Borden is still Borden. When the sports-scribing dodge doesn't crowd me too much, I pick up the little guy and take him to the office with me. Already I believe the newspaper game is in his blood, for the presses and everything about our plant and offices hold him spellbound. He calls Borden the "Funny Man" and laughs delightedly at his tirades.

When we get a chance, the little guy and I visit Tom Layton. The little guy loves Tom's marvelous airplane stories, and twice Tom has arranged for the three of us to take a ride in the plane of a pilot friend. These flights have been sheer enchantment for the happy little boy and—I admit it—his "Grandpa" Evans as well. The child has done wonders for all of us.

After talking it over several times, Angelo, Janey, and I decided it would be all right for the little guy to go to the gym and see for himself, instead of learning secondhand, that Angelo was a professional fighter. I have been the one to take him each time. The first time, when we walked in, Angelo was working out with Louie, the tough but not-too-bright, snorting and comical old pro, and giving the latter a boxing lesson. The little guy watched gravely until the round ended; then he scrambled into the ring, his small face concerned, and asked Louie if Angelo was hurting him, obviously intending to lend a hand if such were the case.

"Naw!" Louie assured him, and from that moment on the rest of us were certain he never would be a bully.

But make no mistake. All forty-six pounds of him is man. It's a sight to watch him, on one of our trips to the gym, wade fearlessly into Louie or some other battle-scarred old pro, his small fists flying. Then the one under attack will grab him and hold him aloft, and he'll scream with pure joy. These fierce characters are his pals. They, in their gruff way, are as proud of this little guy as they are awed by the legend that is his dad.

The kid's laughing son has his serious side, too. He has accompanied me several times to the cemetery and the graves of his parents. He has stood there for long minutes at a time, looking solemnly up at me, saying nothing. He knows that some day I shall tell him the story of the kid, his father, and Maura, his mother, just as I have set it down here.